the dating games #4:

Prom Date

MELODY CARLSON

Revell
a division of Baker Publishing Group
Grand Rapids, Michigan

Published by Revell
a division of Baker Publishing Group
P.O. Box 6287, Grand Rapids, MI 49516-6287
www.revellbooks.com

Printed in the United States of America

Library of Congress Cataloging-in-Publication Data

Carlson, Melody.
Dating Games. #4, Prom date / Melody Carlson.
pages cm
Summary: "The girls of the Dating Game are back this time focused on the biggest date of the year—the prom—but will they discover their friendship is more important than any one date?"— Provided by publisher.
ISBN 978-0-8007-2130-5 (pbk.)
[1. Dating (Social customs)—Fiction. 2. Clubs—Fiction. 3. Proms—Fiction. 4. Friendship—Fiction. 5. High schools—Fiction. 6. Schools—Fiction. 7. Christian life—Fiction.] I. Title. II. Title: Prom date.
PZ7.C216637Daw 2015
[Fic]—dc23 2015003254

The author is represented by Sara A. Fortenberry Literary Agency.

15 16 17 18 19 20 21 7 6 5 4 3 2 1

the dating games #4:

Prom Date

Books by Melody Carlson

Devotions for Real Life

Double Take

Just Another Girl

Anything but Normal

Never Been Kissed

Allison O'Brian on Her Own—Volume 1

Allison O'Brian on Her Own—Volume 2

A Simple Song

My Amish Boyfriend

Life at Kingston High

The Jerk Magnet

The Best Friend

The Prom Queen

The Dating Games

The Dating Games #1: First Date

The Dating Games #2: Blind Date

The Dating Games #3: Double Date

The Dating Games #4: Prom Date

Dating Games Club Rules

1. We will honor the secret membership of the DG.
2. We will be loyal to our fellow DG members.
3. We will help fellow DG members to find dates with good guys.
4. We will report back to the DG regarding our dates.
5. We will not be jealous over a fellow DG's boyfriend.
6. We will never steal a fellow DG's boyfriend.
7. We will abstain from sex on our DG dates.
8. We will not lie to the DG about what happens on our dates.
9. We will never let a boyfriend come between DG members.
10. We will only admit new DG members by unanimous vote.

I'm so envious, I could spit," Bryn declared.

"Just don't spit in here, okay?" Emma teased. The six Dating Games friends were seated at a big corner table in the airport restaurant, waiting for their pizza to be served. It was the last Friday in February, and the plan for the afternoon, arranged by Cassidy, was to give Emma and Felicia—the winners of the Project Santa Sleigh competition—a nice little send-off party before they boarded the nonstop jet to Los Angeles. Emma was so excited that she wasn't even sure she could eat a whole slice of pizza, but she would at least pretend to enjoy it. Mostly she was just happy to be here with her friends. "Honestly," she told Bryn, "I wish you *could* go. I wish you all could go."

"Well, I'd give anything to be in your shoes," Bryn confessed.

"Really?" Felicia's dark eyes twinkled as she stuck out a foot. "You like these flip-flops, do you? Wanna trade?"

"Or maybe these?" Emma held up a foot. She knew that Bryn wouldn't be caught dead in her practical walking sandals.

Bryn gave them both a tolerant smile. "Well, I didn't mean *literally*. But I have been wondering why I didn't try harder to win the Project Santa Sleigh contest myself."

"Like that was going to happen," Abby taunted. "Get real."

"But the red carpet! At only the biggest celebrity event of the year—*the Oscars*!" Bryn moaned dramatically as she pointed at Emma and Felicia. "And you two aren't even *into* fashion."

"Thanks a lot." Emma feigned offense.

"Sorry." Bryn looked slightly contrite. "That was my jealousy talking."

Emma gave her a sympathetic smile. It was ironic that someone as put together as Bryn could be jealous of Emma and Felicia.

"It's okay," Felicia told Bryn. "Everyone knows that I'm seriously fashion challenged. If you hadn't helped me pack yesterday, I'd probably look like a total loser down in LA this weekend."

"I'm not trying to be mean." Bryn sounded like she was backpedaling now. "But you guys know me—I'm the one who obsesses over fashion and style and all that 'shallow' stuff." She rolled her big blue eyes.

Emma chuckled, remembering Bryn's New Year's resolution less than two months ago. Bryn had resolved to stop being so superficial, but she obviously still had a long road ahead. Who could blame her for feeling bummed, though? Winning this amazing trip to Hollywood had pretty much blown Emma's mind. She still could barely believe they were really going.

"Excuse me, Bryn," Abby interjected. "I might not be an obsessed fashionista like you, but I happen to care about style too, thank you very much. I feel a little bummed about not going."

"What about me when it comes to appearances?" Devon demanded. "I'm not exactly slumming here." She held her head higher, pausing to pat her auburn curls. "I care about my looks too."

"Hey, ladies, we're not here to argue over fashion." Cassidy picked up her soda, lifting it high for a toast. "We're here to celebrate Emma and Felicia. Here's to them having a great trip to Los Angeles and a fabulous time at the red carpet event." Everyone lifted their glasses, clinking them together and adding individual toasts, which went from serious to silly, until all six of them were giggling.

"You guys are so lucky." Devon playfully punched Emma in the shoulder.

"Luck had nothing to do with it," Cassidy defended. "Emma and Felicia worked hard to win the contest—fair and square."

"That's true," Abby agreed.

"But the kids we helped were the real winners," Felicia said humbly. "Rosa and Roberta and Mindy and Jackson—the best part of that whole project was seeing their faces light up every time we did something with them. That in itself would've been enough of a reward for me."

"Which reminds me, I promised to send the kids photos from the red carpet—just like Isaac and Marcus did from the Rose Bowl." Emma double-checked to make sure she'd put the Family Assistance Center's phone number in the iPhone that Isaac had insisted she borrow. So sweet of him!

"Don't forget to send us photos too," Bryn reminded her.

"Yeah," Devon agreed. "I want the whole trip documented, from beginning to end, so it feels like we're there with you."

"We've already told you a dozen times that we'll keep you posted," Emma reassured her.

"Emma and I have it all worked out," Felicia added. "She'll be the photographer and I'll be the texter. Between the two of us, you should have pretty good coverage. Anything beyond that, and you better just turn on your televisions or watch a live stream."

"Don't forget to snag some selfies," Devon insisted. "We want to see you actually rubbing elbows with celebs—you know, to prove you were really there."

Bryn set her drink down with a dreamy look in her eyes. "I wonder if you'll see Taylor Lautner."

Emma wrinkled her nose. "Seriously? You're still into him? I thought he was, like, *so last year*."

Cassidy laughed loudly as she gave Emma a high five. "Good one."

"Anyway, we'll do our best," Emma reassured Bryn. "And if I happen to see Taylor, I'll set my personal bias aside and grab a pic. Want me to blow him a kiss from you too?"

Bryn frowned at Emma. "Funny."

They continued to laugh and joke until their pizza arrived, and as Emma looked around the table, she couldn't help but be thankful for this group of good friends. It seemed slightly ironic that the Dating Games, a club they'd created to improve their dating life, had brought them closer together as friends. During the past six months their friendships had become more important than dating. Not that Emma cared to admit this out loud.

"I'm so glad you guys came to the airport to see us off," Emma told them as they were finishing up. "It's been great."

Cassidy held up her arm, pointing to her watch. "Speaking of seeing you off, you promised your mom you'd meet her at security by 5:45. That's like, right now."

Emma nodded. "Yeah, but our flight's not until—"

"Boarding time is 6:10." Felicia reached for her bag. "And our gate's in another terminal. Plus security might be busy since it's a Friday. We better go."

Devon blinked. "You sound like you've done this before."

"Lots of times," Felicia told her. "We visit relatives in California about once a year."

"Well, you guys better get moving," Bryn said.

Emma opened her purse, reaching for some money.

"The pizza is on us," Cassidy told her. "Save your money for LA."

All the girls stood, and everyone took turns hugging Felicia and Emma good-bye—acting as if they were going around the world.

"How long are your friends going to be gone?" the waitress asked Cassidy with concerned eyes.

"Just until Monday," Cassidy said brightly.

The waitress chuckled and walked away.

Emma and Felicia waved their last good-byes and hurried toward the security lines with their purses and carry-on bags in tow. Emma hadn't been overly thrilled that her mother was going with them as an escort, but because Felicia's parents refused to let their daughter take this trip without an adult along, Emma had agreed. And even though it meant she and Felicia had to exchange their first-class tickets for coach to cover Emma's mom's airfare, everyone had agreed it was well worth it in the end.

Really, it was better than having Felicia's overprotective mom along with them. Fortunately, she had to stay home with her other two children. The upside of this arrangement was that Emma's mom was lots more laid-back than Felicia's parents.

"There's my mom up there." Emma gestured to where her mom was standing near the end of the security line—a cup of coffee in one hand and her phone in the other.

"I was just about to call you," Mom told Emma as they all got in line together.

"Sorry, we lost track of the time," Emma told her.

"Luckily the line hasn't been very long." Mom tossed the remains of her coffee in the trash container and sighed. "So, girls, are we having fun yet?"

Emma made a face, and Felicia just laughed.

"I feel a tiny bit bad that my ticket ousted you two from your first-class seats." Emma's mom made a slight smirk. "Or not."

"You're so funny," Felicia told her. "I'm glad you're going with us, Mrs. Parks."

"I'm glad too." Emma's mom nodded eagerly. "I'd be even more glad if I got to go to the red carpet event with you as well. But I guess you can't have everything." She patted Felicia on the back. "Just to make this trip more fun for all of us, you can't keep calling me Mrs. Parks. Okay?"

Felicia looked slightly uneasy.

"Please, just call me Susan."

Felicia nodded. "Okay. Susan."

"Even though I'm here to make sure you two darlings don't

get into any trouble, let's just pretend that we're three girls out to have a good time."

Emma refrained from rolling her eyes.

"Hey, it could be worse," her mom reminded her.

Emma smiled. That was actually true. What if Emma's mom was like Devon's mom—a wild and crazy partier who took up with strange men? Now that would be scary. Or her mom could be like Felicia's mom, fretting over everything and insisting that her little girl dress like an eight-year-old. "I'm glad you came too," Emma quietly told her mom as they moved forward in the line.

Mom smiled at her, gently patting her on the back. "I'll try not to embarrass you . . . too much."

"Hey, I just got a text from Marcus." Felicia turned to Emma, holding up her phone. "He and Isaac are parked on the other side of the river, straight across from the airport. They want to watch as our plane takes off. Isn't that sweet?"

"Seriously?" Emma blinked in surprise. Although they'd gone out a few times and she did really like him, Isaac really wasn't her "boyfriend," per se. For him and Marcus to go to this much trouble . . . well, it really was sweet.

"Yeah. Marcus wants to know which side of the plane we're seated on. He wants us to look down while they wave at us from below."

"I think I printed out the seating chart of the plane." Mom fished in her oversized travel bag, pulling out the packet she'd carefully prepared for them a few weeks ago, and sure enough, she had a plane-shaped map. She pointed to a spot. "We're pretty far back. It looks like you girls are on the left, and I'm on the right."

"Great." Felicia nodded as she texted back to Marcus.

"We'll take a selfie to send them once we're seated," Emma told Felicia as they moved forward in the security line. "Tell them to send us one of them down by the river too."

"Good idea." Felicia turned back to her phone. "This is so fun."

"I know." Emma grinned. "Remember how they sent photos and texts to us from their Rose Bowl trip? Acting like they were such superstars? Now we can do the same thing back to them. Cool."

They had reached the first TSA agent, and although Mom and Felicia were ahead of her, Emma realized she needed to get out her ID and boarding pass. She found a rumpled boarding pass, but as she fumbled through her purse for her driver's license, the man in a dark uniform waited with a grim expression.

"I know I have it," Emma nervously assured him as she tore through her previously organized purse, spilling a couple of items onto the floor. She knelt down, gathering up a hairbrush and lip gloss and continuing to dig through her now messy bag. "I'm sorry it's taking so long."

The security guard said nothing, just bounced his pen up and down with what seemed aggravated impatience.

"Oh, here it is." Emma held up her license with a nervous smile. "You don't have to send me back home after all." Ignoring her attempt at humor, he simply studied her ID and boarding pass, frowning intently as if he thought she was carrying weapons of mass destruction in the soles of her sandals.

Suddenly Emma felt extremely uneasy. What if she blew this? What if they did a complete body search and made her miss the plane? Because it was her first flight—and her first time through airport security—her friends had warned her to be careful. Okay, some of it was just good-natured teasing, but some of it was actual advice. Emma was well aware that things could turn ugly if you did something wrong. Like you weren't supposed to joke with the security dudes. Particularly about having weapons or explosives. Not funny. And you didn't argue with them even if you thought they were being unreasonable or stupid. But as she waited for the grumpy-looking man to return her ID and boarding pass, she could feel herself starting to sweat.

Fortunately, she was allowed to move on, but now it was time to dig her Ziploc bag of toiletries from her purse, load her stuff into a plastic tub, and hoist her carry-on onto the conveyor for the X-ray machine. As Emma fumbled with these tasks, not sure which one to do first, she felt a wave of panic come over her. Mom was about to walk through the X-ray machine. But Felicia paused from preparing her own baggage, insisting that Emma go first. Felicia grabbed up Emma's bag and stuff and set it ahead of her own things, coaching Emma as they went.

"It's her first time flying," Felicia explained to a TSA agent. "She's kinda nervous."

"Oh, well, it's not too painful." The woman smiled at Emma. "Now just step up to that line there and wait until I wave you on through the X-ray. Don't worry, we don't bite."

Emma's mouth felt dry as she followed the directions. She stood with her toes on the line, trying not to freak over the idea of being x-rayed. Was it really like Devon had said? Did they actually see you naked? Eventually the woman waved her through.

"Stop and put your feet right on those footprints," she

told Emma. "Hold very still and place your hands over your head like this." She demonstrated. Emma followed her example, holding her breath as she waited for the machine to do its thing, and then the woman waved her on out. Feeling somewhat relieved but still flustered, Emma went over to the other side, watching as Felicia calmly went through the same process.

Finally, they were both gathering their bags and things, hurrying to get out of the way of others now coming through. Felicia made sure that Emma got everything, including the Ziploc bag that she nearly left behind.

"See, that wasn't so bad," Felicia said cheerfully.

"Thank you for helping me." Emma felt relieved to exit the security area, scanning the terminal for her mom and spying her over by a nearby set of benches. "That was much more stressful than I expected."

"Yeah." Felicia slowly wheeled both their carry-on bags as Emma attempted to stuff her toiletries back into her purse, adjusting the purse strap that seemed to have come undone in the X-ray. "You reminded me of my little sister," Felicia said quietly. "Sofia always gets flustered going through security. I try to help her too." Felicia's dark eyes turned unexpectedly sad.

"Are you missing your family?" Emma took her carry-on bag from Felicia, studying her friend's expression and hoping that she wasn't the homesick type. Emma realized how close Felicia was with her family, but what if she regretted taking this trip?

"No . . . no, that's not it. Not exactly anyway." Felicia's brow creased and her lower lip quivered slightly, almost as if she was on the verge of tears.

"What's wrong then?" Emma pulled Felicia aside, looking into her eyes. "I can tell you're upset about something."

"I didn't want to say anything about it, Emma. Didn't want to spoil our trip."

"What is it?" Emma demanded. "You have to tell me."

"It's just that I'm worried about Sofia." Felicia sighed deeply. "It's silly, really."

"You mean because Sofia's been sick?" Emma knew that Felicia's little sister had gone through some bad bouts of flu this past winter.

"Yeah . . . She had some tests earlier this week." Felicia lowered her voice. "For leukemia."

"Leukemia?" Emma tried to take this in. "Really?"

Felicia attempted a half smile. "I'm sure the results will be just fine. They were supposed to come back this afternoon, but Mom didn't hear back yet. I really shouldn't have mentioned it, Emma. Not right before our big trip. The only reason they tested her was just to rule it out."

"You were right to tell me." Emma placed a hand on Felicia's shoulder. "Of course Sofia will be fine. She's just had some stubborn bugs, that's all. I heard this was a bad year for the flu."

"Yeah." Felicia nodded. "That's what my parents keep saying too."

"But I'll be praying for Sofia just the same," Emma promised. "For her to get completely well." As they rejoined Emma's mom, Emma knew that she would keep this promise. She would pray for her friend's eight-year-old sister. Even though she felt certain that sweet little Sofia couldn't possibly have a sickness as serious as leukemia, she also knew that Sofia had missed a fair amount of school this winter. It was high time for Felicia's little sister to get well.

I'm happy for them," Bryn told her friends as they got into her car out in the airport parking lot. She knew her tone didn't sound convincing and, to be honest, she didn't really believe it herself. "I really am. But at the same time, I can't deny that I'm extremely envious. I won't lie to you guys. I really wish I was going too."

"Duh." Devon laughed. "Who doesn't?"

"But just think about it, I was really instrumental in setting up that whole prize package and the competition and—"

"Which is just one more reason you need to let it go." Abby gave Bryn a warning look from the passenger's seat. "Move on."

"But it's like I can't stop thinking about it," Bryn confessed. "I even asked my parents for the money to sneak down there so I could crash Emma and Felicia's hotel room."

Abby just shook her head.

"What a cool idea," Devon said eagerly. "What'd they say? And can they adopt me and send me down there with you?"

"Seriously?" Cassidy sounded disgusted. "You guys would actually do that to Emma and Felicia?"

"Well, I'd ask them first, of course!" Bryn felt defensive as she started the engine. She was just trying to be honest. "And I'd offer to sleep on the floor or a rollaway bed. And I wouldn't expect to go to the actual red carpet event . . . well, unless I could find a ticket and—"

"But that's just wrong," Abby told her. "I mean, it's not like *you* won, Bryn. Why should you get to horn in on it? You wouldn't really go down there, would you?"

"If my parents had given me the money . . . I think I would." Bryn considered this. "Yeah, I definitely would. It would be fun. Just like a big sleepover. Are you telling me you wouldn't like to go down there too—if you could?"

"No way." Abby folded her arms in front of her.

"Me neither," Cassidy declared. "We didn't win the prize, Bryn. Emma and Felicia did. And they deserved it. It would be wrong to push our way."

"Yeah, six girls and Emma's mom in one hotel room for three nights? Imagine the waiting line for the bathroom." Abby waved her finger at Bryn. "And I know how long it takes you to do your hair and makeup. I'm guessing the slumber party would get old fast."

"Especially for them," Cassidy added.

"Well, maybe just Bryn and I should go down there and crash them," Devon said in a teasing tone. "Leave you two party poopers at home."

"Fortunately—for Emma and Felicia—you guys can't afford to crash them." Abby poked Bryn in the shoulder. "And *you* should be ashamed for even asking your parents for the airfare, Bryn."

"Hey, you can't blame a girl for trying . . . or dreaming." Bryn sighed as she stopped for the traffic light. She honestly felt like the LA trip was going to be slightly wasted on Emma and Felicia. Naturally, she had no intention of admitting that to her friends. It looked like she'd already offended Cass and Abby. And of course, Devon would be on board for crashing in on their friends. But that in itself wasn't exactly reassuring. "Well, I do hope they enjoy it," she said as she pulled out of the intersection. "And you're probably right, Abby. With six girls and one mom sharing one room, it would probably get old fast."

"Speaking of six girls in a hotel room, has anyone made plans for spring break yet?" Devon's voice had a slightly mischievous tone. When Bryn glanced at her through the rearview mirror, she could definitely see a glint of deviousness in her dark brown eyes. Or maybe that was just Devon's natural expression.

"What do you mean?" Cassidy asked warily. "Six girls in a hotel room—what are you thinking of?"

"Oh, I just heard that some of my friends, you know, from my old high school—anyway, they're making plans to go to Phoenix for spring break. I could probably go with them, but I'm not sure it's such a good idea. These girls are kinda wild."

"Then it's definitely a bad idea," Cassidy warned her. "Don't go."

"Well, I probably won't. But it got me thinking that a spring break with girlfriends could be fun. And I've never been to Phoenix, but they made it sound pretty cool."

"Why are they going to Phoenix?" Bryn asked.

"Probably because it's warm down there. And not that far away. And one of my friends has grandparents with a condo they can use."

"Oh?"

"Anyway, it got me thinking that spring break's only three weeks away. Not too soon to make plans."

"Really? Just three weeks?" Abby said absently. "Sure doesn't feel like spring around here."

"Even so, I plan to have some fun on my spring break. I'm going to make the most of it," Devon declared in a sassy tone.

"By doing *what* exactly?" Cassidy sounded a bit suspicious. Based on Devon's recent history, Bryn felt a little suspicious too. Devon certainly had a flair for trouble. To be fair, Devon had been trying to turn things around these past few months. Still, Bryn knew that Devon was Devon and more than a little unpredictable at times.

"I'm not suggesting anything stupid or disgusting or illegal," Devon said a bit defensively. "I just thought going somewhere that was sunny and warm—with some of my girlfriends—well, it might be fun." Then she broke into an old song from the eighties, "Girls Just Wanna Have Fun."

The rest of them attempted to sing along, but no one really knew the lyrics, and before long the song ended.

"I think going to a warm, sunny place with girlfriends sounds fun." Bryn turned on her windshield wipers as raindrops began to splatter down.

"According to the weather forecast this rain is supposed to turn into snow later tonight," Cassidy informed them.

Everyone let out a groan.

"This is like the never-ending winter," Abby complained.

"And track practice starts up next week. At this rate, I should buy snowshoes instead of running shoes."

"See why we need to go someplace warm for spring break? Just imagine hanging by a pool, soaking up some sun, eating junk food, relaxing with your friends," Devon said persuasively. "By the way, does anyone have a grandma with a cool condo or beach house, something in a warm place?"

After it was confirmed that none of them had any snowbird relatives with houses to loan, Bryn decided to broach another subject. Something she'd been thinking about for a week or so. "Spring break is only three weeks off . . . but has anyone been paying any attention to the date for prom this year?" Bryn was pretty sure that she'd be the only one aware of this date, but she waited, just in case.

"I think I heard it was sometime in April," Devon tossed out.

"April 17 to be specific," Bryn clarified. "Which is seven weeks away."

"You're already counting how many weeks until prom?" Abby asked Bryn. And then she laughed. "Of course, why should that surprise me? You're probably already making up a campaign to be prom queen."

"I am not!" Bryn narrowed her eyes. "That's totally ridiculous." Okay, maybe not totally. But it sure wasn't anything Bryn intended to admit to.

"So what's the big deal then?" Cassidy asked. "Why are you talking about prom all of a sudden? Have you been asked or something?"

"No, of course not." Bryn turned the car's heat up a notch. "I seriously doubt that *anyone's* been asked yet. But it's not too early to start thinking about it. Because, as Devon pointed out, it's spring break in three weeks. That means that by the time we get back from spring break it will be only three weeks until prom. Three weeks is not a long time."

"A long time for what?" Cassidy asked. "Seriously, what's the big deal? It's just another dance. Why would anyone need more than three weeks?"

"To prepare for prom." Bryn wasn't surprised that Cass would turn into a wet blanket regarding prom. But what about the others? "Seriously, is there anyone in this car who doesn't *want* to go to prom this year?"

"Is this turning into a DG meeting?" Cassidy asked. "Because if it is, it seems like Emma and Felicia should be present."

"And speaking of DG, what about Amanda?" Devon asked. "I realize we've kinda backed off on DG events lately. But is Amanda still in or not?"

The truth was that the DG—as far as a dating club—had quieted down considerably since Christmas. Oh, they had an occasional "meeting," but it was mostly an excuse to do something together outside of school. And so far, for whatever reason, Amanda and Sienna had not been in attendance. Possibly because they had not been invited. But recently, Bryn had realized how much she missed these times with her DG friends. Just sharing pizza at the airport today—although it had been short and sweet—was a good reminder of the strong bonds of friendship that the girls shared.

"I really don't think Amanda or Sienna even want to be part of the DG anymore," Bryn confided to them. "Last time I heard Amanda mention the DG . . . well, it was pretty negative and snooty."

"Good." Cassidy sounded relieved. "I like the DG with just our original members. Plus Felicia. She fits in nicely."

"And six is a good round number," Abby pointed out. "Not too big, not too small."

"So what're you thinking about in regard to prom?" Devon pressed.

"And what's the big deal when it's still seven weeks off?" Abby added.

"Well, I was looking at some websites last week. Reading up about proms. And I've been learning some interesting stuff. Stuff that might be helpful to all of us."

"Like what?" Devon asked with interest.

"Well, for starters, do any of you know that a prom is very similar to a wedding—"

"A *wedding*?" Cassidy demanded. "How on earth can you compare a silly high school dance to a wedding, Bryn? In fact, that makes me really not want to go to prom. Are you serious?"

"Hear me out," Bryn insisted. "The blog I visited said that a girl who's good at planning and preparing for prom will be better at planning and preparing her wedding."

"Well, I don't intend to plan a wedding," Cassidy shot back at her. "Not until I'm at least thirty."

"Not me," Devon said. "I plan to get married by twenty."

"By twenty?" Abby sounded shocked. "What about college?"

"What about it?"

"You *have* to go to college," Cassidy told Devon.

"Says who?"

"Everyone," Abby declared.

"You really do need to go to college," Bryn added. "We all do. But, hey, we were talking about prom, *remember*?"

"Right," Cassidy said sarcastically. "Prom and wedding planning. Do tell, Bryn."

"Okay, I will." Bryn took in a deep breath. "So think about it, you need a special dress for a wedding, right? You need the right shoes and accessories—same is true for prom. And whether it's a wedding or prom, you have to coordinate the guys' ensembles. Their tuxes need to complement our dresses. And there are flowers that need to coordinate too—both for the guy and the girl. Just like a wedding. And, really, there are lots of things. Dinner plans, transportation plans, and—I forgot the most important thing—the promposal."

"Promposal?" Abby echoed. "What is that?"

"Well, you know how some guys go to really great lengths to make a fabulous proposal to get married? Like I saw this one on YouTube where the guy got all his friends to do this amazing parade with music and clowns and little girls twirling batons and all sorts of crazy things. Anyway, his girlfriend just thought they were watching a regular small-town parade, but then she noticed how people in the parade were holding up these letter cards, spelling out the words *Will you marry me?*" She sighed. "It was so sweet."

"So are you suggesting that guys—I mean, the guys at our school, the same guys who aren't particularly motivated to attend dances or date or even talk to girls without a little prodding and even if they do, they're looking over their shoulder to be sure that Mr. Worthington's not watching and—" Cassidy paused to catch her breath. "Are you suggesting that these same guys will actually *invite* girls to prom by setting up elaborate fake parades and flash dances and whatever, just like an over-the-top wedding proposal?"

"They might." Bryn nodded stubbornly. Okay, she knew

it was a long shot. But hadn't their other dances and events been long shots too? Why did Cassidy have to be such a buzz kill? "At the very least they could deliver a balloon bouquet or a singing telegram . . . something special and memorable."

"You've gotta be kidding." Cassidy laughed so loud she snorted.

"Fine. Make fun if you want, but it could happen."

"Seriously, what guy at our school would stage a parade or even a singing telegram to ask a girl to prom?" Abby demanded. "No offense, Bryn, but I think you're losing it."

Bryn didn't appreciate their sarcasm, but decided not to react. There were better ways to spend energy. In fact their negativism made Bryn feel even more determined to invest herself into this year's prom. And if people wanted to call her shallow or superficial for wanting their prom to be fabulous and unforgettable and fun—well, then that was their problem! Bryn was going to do whatever it took to ensure that prom was the biggest event of the school year.

Devon was grateful to still be living with Emma's grandmother. Really, she was. It was much better than living with her mom—more specifically her mom's creepy new husband. Grandma Betty was a good cook and surprisingly fun to talk to, not to mention a pretty decent card player. But sometimes Devon longed for something more. She wasn't sure exactly what it was she thought she was missing in her life. Sometimes she thought it was boys and fun and action. But then she would try to remind herself of where that had gotten her in the past.

So instead of acting on crazy impulses—and possibly derailing her life—she'd been trying to stick with her dial-a-friend plan. It was actually Emma who had come up with this particular plan. And, despite their ups and downs—and there were many—Emma was still the closest thing to a best friend that Devon had ever had. But it was Saturday night, Emma was down in LA, and Devon was feeling antsy.

It hadn't helped much that Emma and Felicia had been sending all these fabulous-looking photos and texts for the past twenty-four hours. From what Devon could see, those two were having a totally amazing time and, like Bryn, Devon couldn't help but feel envious. Which was probably why she texted Em back this afternoon, saying something stupid and snide and admitting that she was bored outta her gourd. And it was probably why Cassidy called her at 5:30, insisting that Devon attend youth group with her tonight. Feeling homebound and stuck and slightly hopeless, Devon had reluctantly agreed to go.

"It's nice to see you going to youth group," Grandma Betty said as Devon emerged from her room at a bit before seven. "And don't you look pretty tonight." She fingered a strand of Devon's wavy hair. "I was just telling my friend Irene that you have the most beautiful hair—the same color as a shiny copper penny, and all natural too."

"Thanks." Devon smiled. No matter her mood, this sweet old woman almost always made her feel better. "Although I'm not convinced that I really *want* to go to youth group."

"But surely it'll be better than spending the evening with an old lady." Grandma Betty grinned. "Or maybe I can entice you to stick around and play some cribbage with me."

"It might be more fun than youth group." Devon wrinkled her nose.

"Really?" Grandma Betty's eyes twinkled. "In my day, we loved going to youth group—that was where you met the best boys."

Devon considered this. "You mean *nice* boys?"

"Oh, I wouldn't go that far." She chuckled. "Unless things have changed in the last fifty years. I can assure you that not all youth group boys were nice back in my day. I doubt it's much different now."

"Probably not." Devon laughed.

"I guess the point is that at least they're trying."

Devon spotted headlights in the driveway. "There's Cass, I better go."

"Have fun!"

As Devon went out to the car, she wondered if it was possible to have fun at youth group. After all, Grandma Betty was right about one thing—there would be boys. Devon wondered why she hadn't considered this before. "What did you do to your hair?" Devon asked Cassidy as she slid into the passenger seat.

"Huh?" Cassidy reached up to touch her brown hair, which looked rather juvenile in two long pigtails, then giggled. "Oh, the braids—I was helping my mom work in the garden all afternoon. I forgot to take them out."

"I'll just call you Pippi Longstocking." Devon frowned at Cassidy's outfit. The plaid flannel shirt and worn jeans weren't too awful, but those black rubber boots—really? "You look just like a farmer. Seriously, that's what you're wearing tonight?"

"It's just youth group," Cassidy glanced at Devon, then rolled her eyes. "*Not* a beauty contest. Although you do look *lovely*." Her sarcasm massacred the compliment.

"Well, excuse me for caring about my appearance." Devon made an exasperated sigh. "I thought that was one of the conditions of being in the DG, Cass. We were supposed to up our game. *Remember?*"

Cassidy just laughed. "Yeah, whatever. Sorry, I didn't have time to change. My mom was trying to kill herself working on our raised beds. She's got a bunch of seedlings she wants to plant next week if thc weather cooperates. Anyway, she looked like she was about to have a heart attack, so I just had to jump in and help. I worked right up until it was time to leave, but at least I washed my hands." She held out a hand for inspection.

"Eww." Devon turned up her nose. "Your hands might be clean, but those fingernails are disgusting."

Cassidy just shrugged. "Yeah, Mom told me I should've worn gloves." She turned to smile at Devon. "Hey, I'm really glad you came. There's supposed to be a new youth pastor tonight and I've been looking forward to meeting her."

"Her? The youth pastor is a woman?"

"Well, she's a co–youth pastor. She's sharing it with Jarrod."

"Oh." Devon extracted her phone from her purse. "I haven't heard from Emma and Felicia in the last hour. Wonder what kind of mischief they're getting into now?"

"Hopefully no mischief."

After Cassidy parked her car in the church parking lot, Devon opened her door to turn on the overhead light then held up her phone to take a picture of Cass. "I'm sending this to Emma." Devon laughed as she texted the message. *Off to YG with Pippi.*

"Ha-ha," Cassidy said wryly. But she did pull down the visor mirror to look at herself. "Well, there's not much I can do about this now. And if I take the braids out my hair will just be all kinky and frizzy."

"Better just leave it," Devon said as they got out of the car. Besides, she thought as she looped her purse handle over a shoulder, walking toward the building with a spring in her step, this meant less competition for the guys.

Devon hadn't been a regular attendee of youth group since middle school. Oh, Emma had talked her into going a time or two, but for the most part Devon was just not that into it. However, as she followed Cassidy into the brightly lit room, she was surprised at how crowded it was—and even more surprised at the abundant selection of guys. Although she recognized a number of them from Northwood Academy, there were several others from her old public high school too. And a fair amount she didn't even know.

They were barely in the room before several guys came directly toward them—including Lane (who Devon knew was into Cassidy) and Isaac (Emma's main crush) as well as Kent (Abby's guy) and Marcus (who had taken DG girls to dances before). She could tell by their expressions that they were glad to see her. And why not?

"Hey, guys," Devon said in a friendly tone. "What's up?"

"Did you see the latest photo from Emma and Felicia?" Isaac held up his phone right in front of Cass to see.

"I just checked my phone and didn't see anything new." Even so, Devon leaned in to see better. "No way!" she cried as she recognized the actress standing between Emma and Felicia. "Is that really—"

"*Jennifer Lawrence!*" Isaac beat her to the punch.

"That is so cool!" Cassidy exclaimed.

With everyone crowded around, it was hard to see much, so Devon fished out her own phone and was soon staring down at the smiling faces of her two friends with Jennifer Lawrence smiling in between them. Go figure!

"Emma said they ran into Jennifer in front of a popular restaurant and she was really normal and nice. She let them grab the selfie before the paparazzi leaped in and took over," Isaac explained. "Emma said they'd been spotting lots of stars this evening—you know, because of the Oscars tomorrow—but this is the first selfie with a real celeb. Pretty cool, huh?"

Devon couldn't believe it. Emma and Felicia were down in Beverly Hills actually rubbing elbows with the stars. She glanced up from her phone to see that the guys were all clustered around Cassidy, talking and joking and laughing. Meanwhile, she was off to one side—and suddenly feeling pretty left out.

She slipped her phone back into her purse then attempted to move back into the clump of friends. Their conversation had shifted, and Isaac and Marcus were talking about something that happened to them at the Rose Bowl a few weeks ago. For a bunch of guys, these boys were pretty chatty. And Cassidy was right in the midst of them, almost acting like she was part of this "good ol' boys' club." That made Devon feel jealous. Why was she the one being left out?

She reached over and gave a playful tug on one of Cassidy's pigtails. "Hey, guys, what d'ya think of our little Pippi Longstocking here?"

Lane broke into a grin. "I was just about to say something, Cass. Nice look you got going there."

"I, uh, I was working in the garden and didn't have time to change," Cassidy said with what seemed like embarrassment.

"Hey, I think you look great." Marcus slapped her on the back. "Real earthy."

Isaac pointed to Cass's feet. "And I really like those boots. Nice touch."

"Seriously?" Devon frowned at him. Was he kidding?

"Yeah. I like it. Kinda country chic," Isaac told her.

"I bet someone like Jennifer Lawrence might dress like this," Kent added. "Very laid-back and cool."

Cassidy's face lit up. "Thanks, guys."

Devon felt dumbfounded. The guys actually *liked* Cassidy's farmer getup? And here Devon had spent more than an hour putting herself perfectly together—and she knew she looked hot. Yet none of the guys seemed to be looking at her much. And none of them were paying her compliments. What was up with that? What was wrong with these guys?

But there was no time to obsess over the strangeness of this because someone up front was announcing that it was time to get started. The music tempo was picking up, and people were starting to sing along as they hurried to find seats. As Devon stood next to Cassidy, who was beside Lane, she felt seriously confused. Was it possible that she didn't understand guys quite as well as she pretended to? Or were these particular guys just really, really weird?

Although everyone around her was singing with enthusiasm, Devon just stood there. It wasn't that Devon was intentionally trying to be obstinate, but she didn't really know these songs. Besides, it felt insincere to sing along to words that she wasn't too sure she believed in. At least that's what she told herself as she kept her mouth tightly shut. As they continued to sing, she looked around the room, trying to see inside of these seemingly happy faces.

Were these kids really as happy as they seemed? Or was this all just an act? Put on your happy mask for youth group night. She glanced at Cassidy and, although Cass seemed happy too, it didn't really strike Devon as insincere. After all, Cassidy was pretty open and up-front about her beliefs. Certainly, the girl wasn't perfect. And usually—although sometimes it took a while—she admitted it when she was wrong.

The guy who'd been leading the singing—a Jarrod somebody—began introducing a strikingly attractive and exceptionally stylish tall blonde woman named Samantha Robertson. "Sam's degree is in psychology." He chuckled. "But don't let that scare you. She's actually quite nice." He paused for them to laugh. "And she's also a certified counselor who gets teens. More importantly, she loves the Lord. Right, Sam?"

Sam nodded, giving the group a big sparkling smile as she told them how glad she was to be a part of the youth group team. "I can't wait to get acquainted with you all individually," she said with enthusiasm. "And I want everyone to know that I'm a really good listener. At least that's what my friends say." She handed the microphone back to Jarrod, and he announced that tonight he was going to do something different.

"I know it will sound a little weird, but hang with me here. I want us to divide up into two groups for a change. Half of us will be with Sam and the other half with me." He made a slightly devious-looking grin. "Guys go with me and girls stay here with Sam."

This was followed by a lot of loud groans and complaints, but Jarrod just waved them off. "Come on, guys, it'll be fun. And we'll all get back together again after we're done." He invited the girls to remain in the youth group room and explained where the guys would meet. Suddenly everyone was moving.

"Come on up front," Sam called out to the girls. "Fill up the front rows here."

Cassidy grabbed Devon by the arm and dragged her to the front row—and way out of Devon's comfort zone. She cringed inwardly as she slumped down in the chair. This was nothing like what she'd expected. Why had she even come here tonight? Was there any way to get out without making a spectacle of herself? Sam was sitting on a stool, smiling happily at the girls seated all around her. Like the pretty princess about to address the peasants. Everything about Sam looked picture-perfect—reminding Devon of Amanda Norton, a girl who'd turned out to be a stuck-up snob.

"I'm so glad to be here tonight," Sam said cheerfully as everyone quieted down. "I've really been looking forward to meeting you girls. And I've actually been praying for you. It's really great to see you face-to-face." She took in a deep breath, pausing for a moment. "I know that some of you—maybe all of you—were disappointed when Jarrod broke us into two groups. To be fair, it was my idea. I wanted to have you girls to myself for one evening. And"—her eyes lit up—"I want to talk about something that I think all you girls can relate to . . . the opposite sex."

Devon could sense the other girls getting more interested now. And despite Devon's nonchalant exterior, she felt a bit more intrigued as well.

"But first I want to tell you a little bit about myself. I hope that if you feel like you know me, you'll let me get to know you." Sam began talking about how she was born in Southern California into what sounded like a perfect sort of home. "But that's how it looked on the outside," she confided. "If you looked inside our house, you'd see how crazy dysfunctional it really was. My dad was a highly functional alcoholic. And my mom was addicted to pain pills. To make matters worse, they fought all the time—and my dad was abusive to my mom.

When I was just five it all blew up, and the police were called in, and I wound up in foster care."

The room was so quiet that Devon could hear the clock ticking. But Sam definitely had everyone's attention. Especially Devon's.

"The upside of that whole mess is that my mom went into a treatment program and began to recover from her addiction. But my dad went his own way and by the time I started school, my parents were divorced. Mom and I were really poor and my dad didn't pay any child support, but at least the fighting came to an end." She paused to look around the room. "Okay, you're probably wondering what this story has to do with the opposite sex, right?"

A few girls nodded, but Devon wasn't even sure she cared. She actually wanted to hear the rest of Sam's story.

"So I grew up without having a dad in the home. And by the time I was about thirteen or fourteen, well, the boys were starting to notice me." She laughed. "I'm sure you guys know how that can be." Some of the girls laughed too, but a lot of them didn't—the girls, Devon realized, who probably weren't being pursued by boys.

"Anyway, I was so starved for male attention—because of not having a dad in my life—that I pretty much devoured the attention that the guys were giving me. And for a year or so, I was running pretty wild. Mom and I had never really gone to church or anything. And my moral compass was pretty much missing . . . or broken. Although I had this inner sense that I was headed for a disaster—and after having seen what a mess my parents had made of their lives, I realized I didn't want to follow their example."

She took in a deep breath and pushed her long blonde hair

over one shoulder. "So—straight out of the blue—I decided to go visit a church that some of the kids at my school went to. I still can't quite remember what prompted me to do that. I mean, it was so out of character. I guess it was just God." She grinned. "And that night, I heard—for the very first time—the gospel message of how God loved me so much that he gave up his Son in order to have a personal relationship with me." She slowly shook her head. "I couldn't really comprehend everything, but it resonated deeply inside of me and I believed it. I gave my heart to God that night. That was ten years ago and I can still say it was the best decision I ever made in my life.

"And here's my main point—and how this relates to the opposite sex, since I know some of you are dying to know—when I came to the full realization that God was my Father, I no longer craved that male attention like I had before. I was able to keep the guys at arm's length." She laughed. "Well, most of the time. But I discovered that God filled that empty spot in my life—a spot I'd been trying to fill with a boyfriend. It was so freeing and good. That's a place that I hope and pray all of you will come to be at. And I'm guessing some of you are already there."

She held out her open palms, like she was extending an invitation. "So now I'd really like to hear from you guys. I want to open this up for Q&A. And since it's just us girls, you can bring up any topic or question you want—and I will do my best to answer you. Okay?"

Although Devon had plenty of questions, she didn't raise her hand to ask a single one. But she did listen carefully to the girls who did. And she studied Sam closely as she answered each one of them with what seemed like fairly honest and open answers. Devon was trying to determine if this young woman was really who shc seemed to be . . . or something else. But for some reason Devon thought that she could probably trust her. Just the same, Devon wasn't really sure what to do with that kind of trust. For some reason it all made her slightly uneasy.

There was little in Emma's life that had ever made her feel particularly special. A petite blonde with a naturally shy personality, she just wasn't the kind of girl who stood out in a crowd. Not like Devon or Bryn could do. They were the flashy DG members—the "headturners." Even Cassidy, with her practical, no-nonsense style, was better at attracting attention than Emma. Abby, with her brains, athleticism, and confidence, always seemed to outshine Emma too. And to be honest, Emma liked it that way. For the most part.

"Don't you want to look glamorous for this?" Felicia asked Emma as they stood together in the hotel bathroom. Felicia was sporting the sparkly red cocktail dress that she'd worn to the Christmas ball last December, and there was no denying that she looked hot.

"It's not like we're going to actually be *on* the red carpet," Emma reminded her. "We'll be sitting in the bleachers, remember."

"I know, but this is the most exciting thing I've ever done." Felicia paused from styling her sleek black hair. "I want to feel like a star too."

Emma studied her image. The blue sundress had been okay for sightseeing today. The weather had been unseasonably warm, plus the dress was just plain comfortable. But compared to Felicia she looked pretty boring.

"You sort of look like a tourist," Emma's mom said from the open bathroom doorway. "Why don't you put on your pretty green dress from the winter ball? It looks so festive and fun on you."

"Yeah," Felicia urged her. "When will we ever have another evening like this?"

Emma frowned at the slightly wrinkled sundress, then giggled. "Okay, you guys talked me into it. Why not?"

Before long, she and Felicia were downstairs in the hotel lobby, snagging a couple of selfies as they waited for their ride. Emma felt like a million bucks as she observed various bystanders curiously watching them then whispering among themselves.

"It's like they think we're celebs," Emma whispered to Felicia.

"Yeah, I'm glad you changed into that dress." Felicia grinned.

"I can't believe we're really doing this," Emma told Felicia as they went out to get into the hired limo that was part of the prize package.

"It seems kinda surreal—like it's all going to fall apart before we get there." Felicia got a worried look. "You've got the tickets, right?"

"In here." Emma patted her sparkly little purse, then, following her mom's direction, questioned the driver to be sure he knew their destination—which was only about a mile away, but too far to walk in fancy heels.

"It might take longer than usual," he explained. "But there's some Evian water back there if you girls need a drink."

"This is so cool." Felicia giggled nervously as she reached for a bottle.

"I do feel like a star," Emma confessed. "And we need more selfies to send to our friends." They took a few moments to get some shots in the back of the limo, holding up their drinks like a toast.

"Here's to a big night," Felicia told Emma as she texted the words to go with their pics. "Hey, here's a message from my little sister. Sofia must've gotten ahold of my mom's phone." She laughed as she read the words. But then, just like that, her smile vanished. "Oh, no."

"What's wrong?" Emma asked with concern.

"It's—uh—I'm not sure."

"What do you mean? What did it say?"

Felicia stared down at her phone. "First Sofia said to have fun. Then she said not to worry about . . ." Felicia held the phone up for Emma to see, pointing to two words that said *looky mia*.

"Looky mia?" Emma tipped her head to one side. "Is that Spanish?"

"*Mija* is." Felicia's brow creased. "But Sofia knows how to spell that." She repeated the message. "Don't worry about my looky mia . . . looky mia." Felicia looked at Emma with a stricken expression. "Do you think she means *leukemia*?"

Emma knew that this had been troubling Felicia. "Well, you knew that Sofia had that test. Maybe she's just concerned that you're still worried."

Felicia slipped her phone back into her little handbag. "Yeah, that's probably it."

As they rode through the increasingly busy traffic, the two girls stopped talking and laughing. Finally, Emma knew she needed to say something. "Let's pray for Sofia," she said urgently. "Let's pray right now, Felicia. That's better than worrying about her."

Sitting there in their sparkly, fancy dresses, the two girls bowed their heads and prayed that Sofia would be well and fine. They had just said "amen" when their driver announced that they'd reached their destination.

"Thanks," Felicia said quietly to Emma as they climbed out.

"And now we are going to have fun," Emma told her. "No more worrying about things we don't really know about. Okay?"

Felicia nodded with a slightly uneasy expression. "Okay."

For the next couple of hours, they sat among the others who were there to watch the actors and actresses as they strode along the red carpet. They laughed and took photos. By the time it was over, and all of the celebs had disappeared into the theater, both Emma and Felicia were ready to call it a night.

"Aren't you girls going to the Oscar party?" a young woman who'd been sitting next to them asked.

"What party?" Emma asked.

The woman explained how a bunch of them were getting together at a bar and grill to watch the Oscars. "You guys can come too."

Emma thanked her, explaining that they planned to watch the Oscars from their hotel. "My mom is waiting for us."

The young woman looked disappointed, but Emma and

Felicia were both relieved to get back into the limo that was waiting to take them back. It had been a long few days and, although seeing all those stars on the red carpet had been exciting, Emma was suddenly eager for it all to be over.

"I don't think I'd be cut out for the lifestyle of a celebrity," she confessed as they were driven back to the hotel.

"Me neither." Felicia had her phone out again.

"Who are you texting?" Emma asked.

"Mama." Felicia kept her head down as she typed furiously. "I want to know what's up with Sofia."

By the time they reached the hotel, Felicia's mother had responded with a phone call. Emma could hear the conversation between them—and she could hear the pain in Felicia's mother's voice.

"I told Sofia I didn't want you to know about this," she said sadly. "I didn't want you to worry."

"So it's true?" Felicia demanded. "Sofia really has leukemia?"

"It's true."

Tears began to stream down Felicia's cheeks, but she kept her voice calm, and Emma placed a comforting hand on her shoulder. "What are they going to do, Mama?" she asked quietly. "Can they help her to get well?"

"She'll start treatments this week. The good news is that we know what's wrong now. And the doctor promises to do everything possible."

Felicia talked to her mom for several minutes. Emma was impressed with how brave she sounded, but when she hung up she crumbled into sobs. Emma hugged her, trying to assure her friend that it would be okay—although Emma had no idea if that was even possible. What did it mean when an eight-year-old got something as serious as leukemia?

• • ● • •

By Monday afternoon, Emma was more than ready to say good-bye to LA. Oh, it had been interesting and fun—but it was also exhausting and noisy and slightly stressful. She could tell that Felicia was anxious to get home too. In fact, her mom seemed the only one reluctant to leave. "Would you want to live in a place like this?" Emma asked as they were riding to the airport.

"I used to think I would," her mom admitted. "Before I married your dad, I had dreams of moving to a big city and living a completely different kind of life."

"Really?" Emma was slightly intrigued. She couldn't imagine her mom living in a place this big and busy.

"Yeah." She nodded. "But then Edward came along, and then you, and I was so busy being a mom and a wife . . . and then having to make a living . . . Well, naturally my girlish dreams had to be set aside." She made a wistful-sounding sigh. "Time to get back to reality, huh?"

Emma felt guilty. She knew that her mom had been totally blindsided when Emma's dad stepped out of the marriage. And she knew that Mom worked hard just to put a roof over their heads and food on the table. And, despite some scholarship help, Edward's college tuition was not cheap either. Not to mention that Dad's child-support payments had been less than regular. No wonder her mom was feeling blue.

"I'll be out of high school next year," Emma said halfheartedly. "You could always move to a big city after I leave for college."

Her mom just laughed. "Tempting . . . but I think that ship has sailed."

Emma glanced at Felicia. She seemed pretty absorbed with her phone. "Any news from home?" Emma asked.

Felicia's mouth twisted to one side. "Mom and Sofia are getting ready to go to the cancer center right now. It's about a three-hour drive and Sofia has appointments tomorrow." She looked close to tears. "They have to leave before I get home."

"Oh, sweetie." Emma's mom reached over to grasp Felicia's hand. "That's too bad. But you must be relieved that your sister is getting into treatment so quickly. I've heard that early treatment like this can make a big difference in the recovery."

"How long will your mom and sister be gone?" Emma asked.

"I don't know. It sounds like it's going to take a while."

"Maybe you can go up there to see your sister on the weekend," Emma's mom suggested.

"Yeah . . . I hope so."

The car got quiet as they rode to the airport. Emma could tell that Felicia was really worried about Sofia, but she didn't know what more she could say to help. She remembered how devastated she'd been when Grandpa died last year. But at least he'd enjoyed a long, full life. Sofia was only eight. What if she died?

"We'll all be praying for Sofia," Emma finally said as their driver exited for the LAX terminal. "I texted Cass and the others last night . . . I mean, the ones who pray. I asked them all to remember to pray for Sofia." Emma hadn't told Devon the sad news yet. Not because she meant to keep it from her, but because she had specifically targeted the friends who believed in prayer. Devon didn't exactly fall into that category.

"Yeah . . . thanks." Felicia nodded sadly. "Prayers are important."

Before long, the three of them were in the security line. As they waited, Felicia quietly coached Emma, reminding her to have her boarding pass and ID ready. "And make sure you know which bag has your Ziploc of toiletries."

When the time came, Emma wasn't nearly as nervous and, to her delight, she passed through all the checkpoints without any serious mess-ups.

"You're an old pro now," Felicia told her as they headed for their gate.

Emma laughed. "Well, thanks to your help."

While Emma's mom went to the restroom, Felicia and Emma took some last selfies to send to their friends. They both tried to smile big and look like they were still having the time of their lives, but when Emma checked the photos, she could tell that neither of their smiles looked completely genuine.

"On our way home." Felicia said the words aloud as she typed. "Can't wait."

• • ● • •

Everyone was quiet as Mom drove them home from the airport. The streets were wet from a recent rain shower and the sun was just going down.

"It's been a real pleasure getting to know you better," Mom was telling Felicia as she slowed down for the Ruezes' house.

"Thank you, Mrs.—I mean, *Susan*." Felicia smiled. "I've enjoyed getting to know you too."

"I'll be praying for Sofia," Mom assured her as she pulled into the driveway. "For your whole family."

"Thank you," Felicia said again.

"See you in school tomorrow," Emma said as she helped

Felicia get her things out of the trunk. She paused to give her friend a quick hug. "It's going to be okay for Sofia. I just know it is."

Felicia just nodded. "Yeah. I think so too."

"Felicia!" Mr. Ruez emerged from the house, eagerly running toward his daughter and scooping her up. "You're home, mija!"

Emma waved, then got back into the car.

"I'm glad her dad was there to meet her," Mom said as she backed up. "Their family is going through a difficult trial."

"At least they're a family." Emma instantly regretted her words and how they sounded. "I mean, it's good that they have each other, you know?"

Mom nodded somberly. "Yeah. I know."

"We're a family too," Emma said quickly. "You and me and Edward."

"We definitely are. Just not the same as Felicia's family."

"But I'm happy for the Ruez family," Emma added. "I mean, it's actually kind of nice that some of my friends come from happy homes. Well, I know they're not all happy—just because their parents are still married. That would be assuming a lot. But I guess it's reassuring that some of my friends' parents seem happy . . . and are still married."

Her mom smiled at her. "It's actually reassuring to me too, honey. Gives me hope."

Emma sighed. "And as weird as it sounds, it's kind of reassuring to have Devon around too."

"You mean because her home situation is similar to ours?" Mom's brow creased with concern.

"To be honest, I did feel like that at first. And there definitely are some similarities. But the stuff she and her mom have gone through—although it's sad and I feel sorry for Devon—it's actually made me really thankful that you're not like that, Mom. I mean, like Lisa."

Her mom smiled. "I'm thankful too. And although I still try to be friends with Lisa, it's not easy. I don't like some of the decisions she's been making. And I keep thinking she'll wake up one of these days and that she'll get back to her old self. But something happens to a woman, Emma, when the husband she loved and trusted dumps her for another woman. It really takes a toll on your self-esteem."

"Yeah . . ." Emma nodded. "I know."

"But it is possible to recover."

"You have, Mom."

Her mom laughed as she pulled into their driveway. "Well, I wouldn't go that far. I think it's an ongoing process. Maybe I should just say I'm in a *recovery* program."

Emma laughed. "Hey, that works." As she gathered her bags and stuff, she felt so glad to be home. The trip to LA had been amazing and it actually had some incredible moments. Plus they'd gotten some awesome photos on the red carpet last night. And she would have some great stories to tell her friends at school tomorrow. Even so, it wasn't the kind of thing Emma would ever want to do on a regular basis. Leave Beverly Hills and red carpets to girls like Bryn and Devon. As she followed Mom into their humble little house, Emma decided that she was—at heart—just a small-town girl. And that was just how she liked it.

Sometimes Abby questioned why she was still a member of the DG. Not because she was overly confident about her ability to get dates—especially since Kent Renner's interest in her seemed to change like the weather—but more due to the increasing number of activities in her life. With track season officially beginning, the spring production from the drama department, and some of the more academic classes in her heavy schedule, Abby was a busy girl. And like her parents had pointed out just last night, Abby probably needed to prioritize her time better.

"It's okay to say no to some activities," her dad had told her during what had felt like a mandatory parental lecture. "Part of growing up is knowing when it's time to prune something from your life."

"Meaning?" she had pressed.

"Well, I'm sure there are some activities that have no bearing on your future."

"What kinds of things?" she persisted.

"Take your dating club—or whatever you call it." Dad frowned with disapproval, and Abby tossed her mother a warning look. Hadn't she sworn her mom to secrecy?

"Sorry, honey. It just slipped out." Mom gave her a sheepish look.

"But my point is, you need to think about where you're going," Dad continued. "If something is taking your valuable time but doing nothing to pave your way toward college, well then, maybe you should reconsider it."

"But Abby can't spend all her high school years obsessing over college," Mom responded. "She should be enjoying life now too."

"Absolutely," Dad agreed. "But part of the enjoyment should be partnered with what's coming up in your future. For instance, sports . . ." He turned to Abby. "You enjoy your sports, don't you? I mean, for the most part."

She shrugged, remembering Dad's disappointment when she'd decided not to play basketball. "I guess."

"Well, I'm just saying that you're growing up, Abby. That comes with more responsibilities to make wise choices. I just want to keep encouraging you . . . that's all."

Abby thanked him, but still wasn't totally sure what he was getting at. Other than the fact that, as always, Dad was less than supportive when it came to her dating. Naturally, he would want her to give up the DG. But that in itself probably made her feel even more defensive and protective of her DG friends. If that meant she'd be über-busy this spring, well, so be it!

If there was one thing that made her want to stick with the DG, it was friendship. The friendships that she'd participated in this year had all become really important to her. For that reason—and that reason alone—she felt like she'd remain committed to the DG as long as the DG existed. And that was exactly why, when Bryn started talking about prom toward the end of their lunch break, Abby recommended a quick DG meeting that same afternoon.

"But I can't be there until after track practice," she told them. "Not until after five."

They agreed on 5:15 at Costello's, and her friends promised to wait for her. "And if you're late, we'll just spend our time making Emma and Felicia tell us more stories about their big Los Angeles trip," Bryn told her.

• • ● • •

Everyone was seated and chatting happily by the time Abby arrived. Bryn held out an iced mocha. "Welcome," she said with a smile.

"Thanks," Abby said breathlessly, taking the vacant seat next to Cassidy.

"So what's this big news in regard to prom?" Bryn asked curiously.

Abby took a drink, pausing to get her bearings. "Okay, first of all, you all have to swear to confidentiality on this." She held up her right hand like she was taking an oath. "Promise?"

They all held up their hands and promised, and then she continued.

"Okay, I was talking to Kent in drama this morning and he said something that caught me by surprise."

"About prom?" Bryn pressed.

"Sort of. Apparently Kent went to youth group on Saturday night."

"Yeah, so did we." Cassidy pointed to Devon.

"Devon went to youth group?" Bryn said in disbelief.

"It was a slow night," Devon told her with a sly expression.

"Anyway," Abby continued. "Apparently the guys and girls broke up—"

"*Who* broke up?" Bryn demanded. "I didn't even know that anyone was going together."

"Abby means we broke into separate groups," Cassidy clarified. "The guys went with the youth pastor and the girls stayed with Sam."

"Huh?" Bryn looked confused. "Sam?"

"Sam's a woman," Devon explained.

"Anyway." Abby tried to get them back on track. "Kent let it slip that the youth pastor—I can't remember his name, but—"

"Jarrod," Cassidy supplied.

"Right. Jarrod. Anyway, Jarrod gave the guys this little talk, and apparently a number of guys were there from Northwood."

"Yeah," Devon jumped in. "Isaac and Lane and Marcus and—"

"Marcus was there?" Felicia said with interest.

"Yeah," Cassidy told her. "And I don't think I've ever seen him there before, but he—"

"Do you guys want to hear this or not?" Abby demanded.

"Yeah, sure." Bryn patted Abby on the shoulder. "Just spit it out, okay?"

Abby rolled her eyes. "Okay. It sounds like that youth pastor, Jarrod what's-his-name, gave the guys the exact same speech that Worthington gave the guys last fall." Of course, she couldn't admit to her friends that her own father was a huge fan of the school's dean of boys. She'd even heard her dad telling her mom that Mr. Worthington was "the greatest thing since sliced bread." Whatever that was supposed to mean.

"About not dating?" Bryn asked.

Abby just nodded as she paused to sip her drink.

"Seriously?" Devon frowned. "That's what Jarrod said to the guys?"

"Well, Kent didn't go into much detail. He just kind of let it slip that because of what the youth pastor said—which seemed to have echoes of Worthington—none of them will be asking girls to prom."

"*What?*" Bryn slapped her hand on the table.

"Then why even have prom?" Devon said with disgust.

"Exactly." Abby nodded eagerly. "That's what Kent said they're going to do."

"Huh?" Emma looked slightly lost.

"Kent said that some of the guys plan to circulate a petition. Starting this week."

"A petition for what?" Cassidy asked.

"Not *for* anything," Abby clarified. "The petition is *against*. The guys want to see prom *canceled*."

"No prom?" Bryn looked truly horrified.

"Can they do that?" Devon asked with concern.

"I don't know," Abby confessed. "But it sounds like they're going to try."

"That's too bad," Emma said. "I was pretty sure that Isaac was going to ask me too. He even hinted about it a few weeks ago."

"Well, Isaac was at youth group that night," Devon told her. "He might be on the anti-prom bandwagon too."

"This is just wrong," Bryn proclaimed. "How can we be the only school that doesn't have prom?"

"It makes me want to go back to my old high school," Devon said sullenly.

"Who do they think they are?" Bryn asked. "Just because a handful of guys are anti-prom doesn't mean the whole school should give it up. I mean, fine, if they don't want to go to prom, let them stay home. Why do they want to spoil it for everyone?"

"I wonder how many signatures they need to get," Cassidy mused.

"Even if they got all the guys to sign, that would only be about 50 percent," Abby pointed out.

"Why would all the guys even sign it?" Bryn asked.

"Because guys always like to complain about events like prom," Emma told her. "I remember how my brother, Edward, would go on about how expensive it was, how it wasn't fair that the guy got stuck with the bill, but it was mostly for the girl."

"Kind of like a wedding." Abby nodded toward Bryn.

"Well, you can't have a wedding—just like you can't have a prom—without guys," Bryn said wryly.

"This is so lame," Devon grumbled.

Emma shook her head. "Is there any way to stop it? What if we circulate our own petition? Mrs. Dorman is our faculty advisor. Maybe we could ask her to put a stop to the boys' petition."

"Isn't that kind of undemocratic?" Cassidy asked.

"Circulating a petition might be like freedom of speech," Abby added.

"Just the same, someone needs to put the kibosh on those

boys," Devon declared. "Before they gain any more momentum."

"You're right." Bryn nodded. "It's time to get really proactive."

"Do you have a plan?" Devon asked.

Bryn's brow creased. "I'm working on it. The most important thing is to act fast. That means some of us need to get onto prom committee ASAP."

"To get onto prom committee, you have to be a student council representative or else appointed by one," Abby pointed out.

"You're a representative," Bryn said back. "You could be on prom committee."

"No way." Abby firmly shook her head. "With track and the play coming up, I don't have time."

"I'm a student council rep too," Cassidy admitted.

"Great," Bryn told her. "You and I will both volunteer for prom committee and then we'll appoint one or two DG members."

"But what if I don't want—"

"Cassidy," Bryn said sharply. "Are you going to let your fellow DG members down?"

"But I really don't want to be on prom committee."

"It'll look good on your college application," Abby told her.

Cassidy seemed to consider this. "Who would I appoint—I mean, if I was on the committee?"

"Not me," Devon told her. "I'm auditioning for the play too. And I expect to snag a big part."

Cass looked hopefully at Emma. "What about you?"

Emma just shrugged.

"You're artistic," Bryn reminded Emma. "You'd be a real

asset on the decorations committee. Maybe you could head it up. That would look good on your college app too."

"I guess if Cass does it, I could too." But Emma looked less than enthused.

Bryn turned to Felicia, who was looking down at her phone with a furrowed brow. "What about you, Felicia? You could help Emma with—"

"What's wrong?" Emma suddenly asked Felicia.

Felicia looked up with tears in her eyes, but said nothing.

"Is it about Sofia?" Emma pressed.

Felicia just nodded with a trembling chin, like she was on the verge of tears.

"What happened? Is she okay?" Emma's eyes grew wide.

"Yes . . . it's just a problem . . . with her treatment." Felicia looked back down at her phone. "Something unexpected."

"I already told most of you that Felicia's little sister Sofia was just diagnosed with leukemia," Emma said. "She's only eight years old. She's at the pediatric cancer center with her mom right now." Emma turned to Felicia. "But what's wrong?" she asked gently. "What's the problem with her treatment—the unexpected thing?"

"It's just that our insurance—it doesn't cover the cancer center where Mom took Sofia for treatment. And it's the best treatment center in the state and for miles around. They said she has to—to leave." Felicia really did start to cry.

"Well, that's just wrong," Emma proclaimed.

"That is totally wrong," Bryn agreed. "How can they do that?"

"Where will Sofia get her treatment then?" Emma quietly asked Felicia.

"My mom has some names of other places . . . places that

are farther away . . . where our insurance will cover it. But none of them are as good as where Sofia is now."

"Why can't she just stay there?" Cassidy demanded. "Why should your insurance get to decide what's best for her? Why can't your parents decide?"

Felicia sighed. "That's the way it is."

"But they have no right to turn her away," Emma argued. "This is a free country, isn't it? Why can't people get treatment from the place they believe is best?"

"Because . . . without insurance . . . it's too expensive." Felicia wiped her tears with a napkin. "We can't afford it."

The table got very quiet now. Abby felt seriously indignant for Felicia's sake. How was it fair that good medical treatment could be denied to a child—just because her family had the wrong insurance provider, or simply didn't have enough money? It was so unjust.

"I have an idea to save our prom," Bryn said suddenly.

"Seriously? Are you still obsessing over prom?" Abby could feel the irritation in her tone. "What about Sofia?"

"This is for Sofia too." Bryn's brows arched mysteriously. "A way to help her."

Suddenly every girl at the table gave Bryn her full attention.

"We'll turn prom into a fund-raiser," Bryn began. "I'm not totally sure how, but I'm sure it can be done." She twisted her mouth to one side. "For starters we'll raise the price of tickets—"

"But that will turn the guys totally against it," Devon told her.

"Not if all the proceeds go to help someone in need."

"But proms are expensive," Abby pointed out. "Ticket proceeds help to cover the cost."

"Unless we got some sponsors and some donations from businesses." Bryn rubbed her chin. "Maybe I'll go to the Hartfords again. They're the richest people I know. And they really care about kids and our school. They might be willing to help again."

"I still don't quite see what this has to do with Sofia," Emma complained.

"Or how you plan to pull this off," Cassidy said with skepticism.

"Okay, let's start at the beginning. We'll be on prom committee," Bryn started to explain. "Cass and Emma and me to start with. By the way, the first meeting is tomorrow after school, which means we need to get busy before then. At tomorrow's meeting we'll vote to raise the price of prom tickets and to turn prom into a fund-raiser." She held up a forefinger. "Hey, maybe we could even have some other fund-raising events related to prom. And then, when it's all said and done, all the proceeds will go to Sofia's cancer treatment." She beamed at them. "How about that?"

Felicia's dark eyes lit up. "Really? You would do that? Donate all the proceeds to my little sister's treatment?"

Bryn nodded firmly. "You bet we would. We want to help your sister. And turning prom into a fund-raiser would be a great way to raise money."

Abby was getting some mixed feelings right now. On one hand, she loved the idea of helping Felicia's little sister. On the other hand, was Bryn just being opportunistic? Was she using this little girl's very serious cancer diagnosis to garner enthusiasm for a prom that was in peril of perishing—and perhaps should be quietly buried?

But suddenly everyone was talking at once and it was clear

that they were enthusiastic and supportive of the fund-raising prom idea. And Bryn was so excited about the possibilities. Abby knew this wasn't the time and place to question her best friend's true motives. Besides, how would it look to sound so negative and suspicious with Felicia so obviously thrilled by this idea? Talk about being a wet blanket. Abby decided to just keep her mouth shut.

Sometimes Bryn felt like she'd make a good general. Not in a real army, of course, but she was good at leading the troops. And by the time she got home from the DG meeting, she was already preparing her battle plan. First she texted Emma and Cassidy, reminding them of tomorrow's prom planning meeting, as well as assigning them tasks to have completed before the important meeting. After dinner, she called Mrs. Hartford, leaving a long message that explained her idea to turn prom into a fund-raiser for Sofia Ruez.

"Everyone knows how prom can be considered such a selfish and shallow sort of event," she said finally. "And I know how much you and Mr. Hartford believe in Northwood Academy—how you respect the school's traditions and care about the students. I just think we could all do something really amazing this year. Similar to what we did with Project Santa Sleigh. Feel free to call me or text me or even use email to let me know if I can count on you for support. And, even if you are unable to partner with us on this, I just want to thank you again for all your support in the past. We really appreciate you." Then she said a cheerful good-bye and hung up.

First thing on Wednesday morning Bryn went to Mrs. Dorman's office, since she was the staff member overseeing prom. She signed up herself, Emma, and Cassidy for prom committee.

"I'm glad to see you taking interest in this," Mrs. Dorman told her. "Last year it was like pulling teeth to get students to help with prom."

"Well, I believe in keeping traditions like prom alive," Bryn assured her. "And I've heard rumors that there are some kids in our school who don't feel the same."

Mrs. Dorman's brows arched. "Really?"

Bryn nodded. "Yes. Some students would like to destroy our prom."

Mrs. Dorman looked worried. "Have there been threats of some kind? Some sort of danger I should be aware of?"

"Well, it's not exactly dangerous. It's more of an anti-prom campaign."

"Oh . . ." Mrs. Dorman nodded with a slightly concerned expression. "Perhaps I should attend this afternoon's meeting myself."

"Yes," Bryn agreed. "That's a good idea."

By midday Wednesday, the guys had already gathered several pages worth of signatures on their anti-prom petitions. Enthusiasm for a prom boycott seemed to be spreading like wildfire—and Bryn was ready to break out a fire extinguisher. But she knew she needed to pace herself, to go about this carefully. And from what she could see, after sneaking a peek at Kent Renner's petition list outside of the math department, it was mostly guys who were signing those stupid papers.

"This is brilliant, dude!" A boy who was only a freshman, and probably had no intention of attending prom this year, gave Kent a victorious fist bump. "I remember how much cash my brother dumped to go to his prom last year. I told him he should've just piled his money in a big heap in the backyard and lit a match to it." The kid laughed like this was hilarious.

Kent just nodded as he took back his pen. "Good point, bro. It's a lot of cash for just one night."

Bryn had simply bitten her tongue. Of course, the cheapskate boys would be thrilled about a prom boycott. But there had to be some guys who appreciated tradition—the kind of fellow who could enjoy an unforgettable night with a pretty girl on his arm. Where were these boys?

By the end of the day, Bryn was ready to explode. If these guys thought they could undo years of Northwood tradition just by circulating a stupid petition—well, as her grandpa would say, they had another think coming! She knew she needed to reserve her opinions for the prom meeting after school today. But it wasn't easy keeping her mouth shut.

"Did you make the poster?" Bryn asked Emma as they met in the breezeway outside of the library. The meeting was scheduled in the library's conference room.

"Right here." Emma patted the oversized folder. "I got a really good photo of Sofia from Felicia."

"And I just sent the article to the school's website," Cassidy told her. "Including a photo of Sofia. It should be up any minute now."

"Great." Bryn gave them a thumbs-up. "Ready for battle?"

"Battle?" Emma frowned.

"You've seen the petitions circulating," Bryn reminded her. "The guys are thinking they've got this all wrapped up."

"Lane admitted that they'll be represented at the meeting too," Cassidy said as they walked through the library.

"I figured as much." Bryn turned to face her friends. "And remember what I told you guys, don't just nominate me for committee chairperson, but say something about why I'd be a good chair, okay?"

"Something besides the fact that you'd like to be prom queen?" Cassidy said in a teasing tone.

"You know that's not true." Bryn frowned.

"You're sure about that?" Cassidy questioned her.

"Absolutely." Bryn firmly nodded. "I just happen to love traditions. You guys know that. And I love the idea of raising funds for Sofia's treatment." She looked directly at Cassidy. "Don't you?"

"Of course." Cass sounded defensive.

"And . . ." Bryn paused to see if anyone was near enough to eavesdrop. "I wasn't going to tell anyone until we were in the meeting, but I got a text back from Mrs. Hartford and their foundation is very interested in participating with our fund-raiser."

"Seriously?" Emma's eyes grew wide. "That's awesome, Bryn."

Even Cassidy looked impressed. "Nice work!"

"Thanks." Bryn smiled as she pushed open the door to the library. "So I really need you two to step up at this meeting. Nominate me with real enthusiasm, okay?"

They both agreed and, feeling like she was leading her troops, Bryn headed for the library conference room. But, to her dismay, there were only a few students in the room.

All girls and all preoccupied with their phones or books and not looking as if they really cared much about this meeting. Maybe that wasn't even what they were there for. Plus Mrs. Dorman hadn't arrived.

"This is where the prom committee is meeting, isn't it?" she asked brightly.

"Uh-huh," Mazie Tucker answered without looking up from her iPhone.

"Have a seat," another girl said.

"Let's sit up here." Bryn led her friends to the other side of the room, placing her hand on the chair at the head of the table. "We'll save this for Jason. I assume since he's student council president, he'll want to chair this meeting." She lowered her voice, winking at them. "At least to start with anyway."

It wasn't long until a few other girls straggled in, and eventually Mrs. Dorman slipped into the back of the room, taking a seat against the wall with her notepad in hand.

"It's past 3:30," Bryn pointed out. "I wonder if we should go ahead and start the meeting since—"

"Here we are!" Jason announced like he was the star of the show. He had several of the guys with him—the same ones who'd been circulating the anti-prom petitions—and they ceremoniously entered the room. It was amazing how everything got noisier and busier when boys got involved. Not that Bryn was opposed to that. Not at all. The best-case scenario would be for lots of guys to get involved in prom committee. And she hoped she'd be able to entice them to consider that today.

"This chair for me?" Jason said as he made his way up front. Meanwhile the other guys remained clustered back by the door. Jason grinned at Bryn with a devious twinkle in his eyes. "Thanks, Bryn."

"No problem." She smiled back. "Glad you could make it. We were about to start without you."

Jason held up a stack of messy-looking papers—obviously the signed petitions. "Well, that's not necessary." He looked around the room with a smug expression. "In fact, this whole meeting might be unnecessary."

"And why is that?" Bryn asked innocently.

He waved the papers in the air. "Because this might just be the year when we finally put to death a silly and expensive tradition that has obviously outlived its usefulness."

The other girls were watching him with quiet interest and what Bryn hoped might be concern. Surely they didn't want to see their prom kicked to the curb.

"So are you calling this meeting to order?" Bryn calmly asked Jason.

"This is not a student council meeting," he reminded her.

"I know. It's a prom planning meeting. That's why we're here. To plan prom." She forced a bright smile. "So why not get on with it?"

He waved the pages again, but this time his eyes were focused on Mrs. Dorman. "Unless the majority of students at Northwood don't want a prom. Do we need a meeting then?"

"Why don't you explain?" Mrs. Dorman told him.

"What about nominations for prom committee chairperson?" Bryn stood up, facing Jason with defiance. "Shouldn't we do *that* first? Before we bring anything to the table—shouldn't we have an official prom chairperson appointed? To keep the meeting in order?"

"Unless we're *canceling* prom." Jason gave her a sly grin.

"He can't just walk in here and cancel prom, can he?" Shc directed this to Mrs. Dorman. "Does a student council president have that kind of authority? Shouldn't it be put to the vote?" She shot a worried glance at Emma and Cass.

"This is no different than a vote." He rattled his silly papers dramatically. "By the end of the week, we'll have the majority of students signed off on this. And, hey, the people have spoken."

"But that's not fair," Bryn protested. "The majority of students don't even *go* to prom."

"One more reason it's becoming obsolete."

"That's just your opinion."

Jason shook the papers in her face now. "And the opinion of close to two hundred other Northwood students. And that was just one day's worth of signature gathering. At this rate we should have a majority by noon tomorrow."

"But why should the *majority* decide?" Bryn demanded.

"Really?" Jason put his hand to his chest like he was appalled. "You oppose democracy now? You want to turn Northwood into a dictator state?"

"No, of course not! I just mean that the prom is for juniors and seniors and it doesn't make sense that everyone—"

"*All* students will be juniors and seniors—*eventually*."

"It seems to me that you're the one who's opposing democracy, Jason." Bryn shook her finger at him. "Otherwise, you'd allow the whole student body to vote on this." Bryn looked at her friends, wishing for some help or support, but both of them were distracted with their phones. What was wrong with them?

"Signing a petition is the same as a vote!" he proclaimed.

"But it's not a valid vote—and it's not even fair!" Bryn slammed her palm down on the table with a loud bang.

"All right, all right." Mrs. Dorman stood, holding up her hands. "As much as I appreciate your enthusiasm, this meeting is not meant to be a debate. As your faculty advisor I'm suggesting you conduct yourselves in an orderly fashion. Treat this like an official meeting."

"How about if we begin with chairperson nominations?" Cassidy suggested.

"But why appoint a chair if there's not going to be a prom?" Jason asked her.

"Because we do not know for certain that prom is being canceled," Bryn told him in a calm but firm voice. "And until we know that for sure, it seems reasonable to proceed with chairperson nominations."

"I nominate Bryn Jacobs," Emma said suddenly. And setting her cell phone aside, Emma stood up. "Bryn has shown that she's responsible. And we know she's experienced because of the good work she did on the Christmas ball. Bryn is the kind of girl who really cares about school traditions. Besides that, Bryn has come up with a really unique idea that could turn our prom into something that's much more than just a formal dance." Emma locked eyes with Bryn then sat down.

"I second the nomination," Cassidy declared. "Bryn is the best person to chair prom. Not only does she care about the quality of this event, but like Emma said, she's got a plan to make it into something really great."

Bryn smiled at her friends. They didn't let her down after all.

"I nominate Jason for the chair," one of the guys in back yelled out.

"But he doesn't even want prom," Bryn pointed out.

"I second the nomination," another guy called out.

Bryn did a quick head count. If this turned into guys against girls, Jason would win.

"Are there any other nominations?" Mrs. Dorman asked.

"I nominate Lane Granger," Bryn said suddenly. Okay, it was a long shot, but it could work. "The reason I'm nominating Lane is because I honestly think he would be more supportive of prom than Jason." She smiled at Lane and to her relief, he smiled back.

"I second the nomination," Cassidy said.

If only this would split the guys' vote. In that case, Bryn would win.

"Are we ready to put this to a vote?" Mrs. Dorman asked.

Before anyone could answer, the doors to the conference room flew open and Felicia and Devon burst into the room, followed by several more girls. Bryn wasn't sure what was going on, but when she looked at Emma and Cass, they both held up their phones as if the answer lay there. Of course, they had texted more girls in the school, probably begging them to come to this meeting. Brilliant!

"I think we're almost ready to put it to a vote," Bryn told Mrs. Dorman. But first she brought the latecomers up to speed, explaining how Jason had shown up with the intent of throwing their prom under the bus. Bryn pointed at the petition papers in his hands. "Jason feels that just because the guys have gathered a bunch of signatures, they have the authority to take prom away from us." She looked at the girls clustered in the back of the room. "But I don't think that's fair. Prom is a time-honored tradition in this school. Something that we all look forward to. And, sure, there might be some outdated things in regard to prom, but let's not toss it all aside. I happen to have some ideas that could transform prom into something truly amazing. But if Jason has his way, we'll never have the chance."

"And for that reason you can all thank me." Jason made a mock bow. "Seriously, who has time for this? Has anyone considered how many hours it takes to make the preparations for prom? Have you thought about the expense? What it costs the school too? Couldn't that money be put to better use? Has anyone taken a good look at some of the sports uniforms lately? But that's not all, what about what it costs us guys to take a chick to prom? I don't know about you guys, but I can think of better ways to spend my money. For the cost of prom, I could probably buy a—"

"Speaking of money," Bryn cut him off, "I want to share with everyone how I think prom could change." She reached for Emma's poster, holding it up. "This little girl is the sister of one of our students. Her name is Sofia and she's just eight years old. Sofia was recently diagnosed with leukemia. Her family took her for the best treatment at the best pediatric cancer center in the area, but they soon found out their insurance won't cover it." She paused for dramatic reasons, holding the poster high so everyone could see this sweet little girl's big brown eyes. "The quality of Sofia's treatment could be the difference between life and death for this little girl. Think about it. About eight years from now, where will Sofia be? Will she be right here, enthusiastically helping to plan her own prom . . . or will she be gone?"

Bryn looked imploringly at the faces around the room. "We have the power to turn our prom into a fund-raiser. A fund-raiser that could help save this sweet little girl's life by getting her the kind of medical treatment she needs. We have the power to help save a life." She turned to Jason. "If that's a bad way to spend your money—well, then you're just not the guy I thought you were."

Jason looked totally off guard, just staring at the poster.

"Look, I understand why you guys are so anti-prom," Bryn continued gently. "It *is* expensive. But think about it—what if the proceeds from your tickets all went toward Sofia's treatment expenses? Would that change your thinking at all?"

No one said anything, but some of the guys looked slightly less smug. And when Mrs. Dorman suggested they put the chair position to a vote, Bryn won easily. Not only did all the girls vote for her, but a couple of the guys did as well. However, the disagreement did not appear to be over as Jason and several of his buddies quietly exited the conference room and the real planning meeting began. Bryn suspected by Jason's expression that he wasn't ready to give up yet. But for the moment, she was pleased.

By the time the prom meeting was over, Cassidy was glad she'd agreed to help out. And she felt genuinely proud of Bryn. It was amazing to think that Bryn had gotten the Hartfords to offer matching funds for whatever was raised at prom. If they could just get prom attendance up, it could end up being a significant chunk of change for the Ruez family. Cassidy had actually played with the numbers a bit, and even if it wasn't enough by itself to keep Sofia in the best pediatric cancer center, it would make a difference. And if Bryn hadn't made such a great argument today, prom could've easily gone down without a fight.

"Once again, I have to admit I was wrong," Cassidy told Emma as she drove them home from school.

"Wrong about what?"

"Bryn. I misjudged her again. When she started putting together that plan to turn prom into a fund-raiser, I was worried it was just her way to get herself into the limelight so that she could run for prom queen. But it seems like she really invested herself today . . . like she really cares about Sofia."

"Yeah, I think she does." Emma poked Cassidy in the arm. "And you were pretty great today too, Cass."

"Huh?"

"Your idea to text our friends and get them into the meeting like that. Those extra votes made a difference."

"Yeah, and it was nice that Mrs. Dorman didn't dismiss them for not being student council representatives."

"I think Mrs. Dorman secretly wanted to make sure prom happened," Emma said.

"Well, like Bryn pointed out, everyone is a member of the student body. Everyone should have a vote and a say about it. Besides, we could've appointed them to the prom committee if we'd wanted to. If they want to help."

"Bryn's going to need lots of help," Emma said as Cassidy pulled into her driveway. "I mean, if she really thinks she can get kids to dole out that much money to go to prom. I know that it would stop me from going if I had to pay my own way."

"Yeah, but what about Bryn's idea that prom tickets include dinner? That saves some money," Cassidy reminded her. "If you think about it, that makes it kind of a bargain."

"That's assuming people were going out to dinner." Emma grabbed her stuff. "Some people just do their own meals at home. You know, like we've done for other dances."

"That's true." Cassidy frowned. "But that's a lot of work too. It might be kind of fun to have dinner catered by someone else."

Emma gave Cass a sly look. "Meaning you're already planning on going?"

Cassidy shrugged. "Hey, if I got asked . . . I might want to go . . . if it was the right guy anyway."

"You mean like Lane?" Emma teased.

Cass frowned. "Except didn't you notice that Lane was in Jason's anti-prom group? And he didn't even stick around for the meeting after Bryn won the vote."

"Neither did Isaac." Emma sighed as she opened the car door. "And I honestly thought that, of all the guys, Isaac might be the first one to break the guy code and ask me to prom."

"Well, if things work out how Bryn hopes, maybe he will."

Emma climbed out and waved. "See ya."

As Cassidy drove away, she wondered why she suddenly cared about going to prom anyway. Really, did it matter? Oh, sure, it would be fun if Lane asked her. But she had no intention of asking him. And she didn't want anyone in the DG to try to set her up either. Hadn't they all agreed that this time—it was up to the boys to do the asking? Well, she didn't know about the rest of the DG, but Cassidy was determined to stick to her guns. If Lane didn't invite her, she was content to stay home.

When she got home, Cassidy went online to see if her article had been uploaded onto the school's website yet. Not only was it posted, but there were a number of comments as well. Most of them were positive and supportive, but there were a few from some of the disgruntled guys. Including, she was surprised to see, one from Lane.

It's nice to see the prom committee cares about helping others and I have to agree that Sofia Ruez's leukemia treatments are a worthwhile cause. But I want to challenge the prom committee. What if you just held a plain old fund-raiser—something we could all get behind? Why do you have to attach the fund raising to an event that most of the student body doesn't even want to attend? What if you created a more inclusive event that invited everyone to participate? Wouldn't you raise more money to help Sofia? Just saying.

My Two Cents,
Lane Granger

Cassidy read Lane's post a couple of times and, despite herself, she thought it made real sense. In fact, she totally agreed with him. At the same time, she realized that she was on the prom committee. She was supposed to be supportive of prom. And if she told Bryn her concerns, she might be considered the enemy.

Cassidy wrestled with this for a bit and finally decided she didn't care if she offended Bryn. The truth was the truth and what was right was right. In this case, even if it meant sacrificing prom, she felt that Lane really was right. So she shot off a comment to the school's blog, admitting that she agreed with Lane. Then, to avoid feeling two-faced, she sent Bryn a quick text, suggesting she check out the prom comments on the school's website. Okay, she felt a little guilty when she hit Send. But, hey, she was just being honest . . . and true to herself. And the sooner Bryn knew it, the better it would be for everyone.

Cassidy felt a sense of relief as she helped her mom to get dinner ready. She'd never been that enthused about being on prom committee in the first place. But she was glad to help with a fund-raiser for Sofia.

"Is that your phone?" Mom asked as Cassidy was chopping a tomato.

Cass paused to hear her phone beeping, and a quick check revealed that the text was from Bryn. She did not sound happy.

What do u mean? Answer phone. Now.

Suddenly Cass's phone was jingling. Of course, it was Bryn. "Hey, Bryn." Cassidy made an apologetic smile to her mom, stepping into the laundry room. "What's up?" she asked innocently.

"That's what I want to know. I feel like I just got stabbed in the back. By a friend too."

"Sorry, but when I read Lane's—"

"You're on *prom committee*," Bryn said sharply. "We're supposed to be on the same team. I was counting on you, Cass. What about Sofia?"

"I'm still on board for a fund-raiser, but—"

"You betrayed us when you wrote that comment on the school's blog, Cass. Everything we worked for today—you just blew it all off. And you were there, you saw how hard we worked to gain what little ground we got. I can't believe you're undermining prom like this."

"Am I not allowed to have my own opinion?" Cassidy demanded.

"Of course. As long as you agree with me."

Cass laughed. "Yeah . . . right."

"So you don't want to help Sofia?"

"You know I do. But I think Lane is right. I think we can help her more if we hold an event that everyone in the school can come to—something they'll all want to attend."

"That's your opinion, Cass. That doesn't mean it will happen."

"Why not? We've had successful fund-raisers before. Why not with this? We could come up with something to sell tickets for. Maybe a concert or—"

"Even if you came up with another idea, do you honestly

believe you could charge as much as we could do with prom tickets? Everyone *expects* prom to be expensive. That's the guys' biggest gripe. Remember?"

"Yeah, and their gripe is getting more legit, Bryn. We just voted to raise the price of tickets. Remember?"

"Yeah, but we're offering them dinner too. Remember? And I already found some possible sponsors to donate food items too."

Cassidy frowned at the washing machine. How did she get involved in this in the first place? Arguing over a prom she really didn't care if she attended? *Really?*

"I was so proud of you today, Cass. The way you texted the other girls—that was so brilliant. Getting everyone into the meeting to hold off Jason. I felt like I could really count on you."

"You *can* count on me. But not to be your puppet. I do have my own opinions, Bryn. And the whole idea of prom has always felt kind of exclusive to me. Remember when we were freshmen and sophomores—didn't you feel a little left out when you overheard everyone talking about prom like they were going off to some secret society? You see all the posters and stuff, but you know you're not allowed to go. I mean, really, that was one reason we agreed to start the DG last fall. To ensure we didn't miss out on stuff like this."

"Exactly. Isn't that what we're doing?"

"But I feel bad for other people. What if they still feel like we did? Left out, sitting on the sidelines."

"They just have to wait until they're older. And besides, sometimes the younger girls get asked. Remember when Ashley Marsh—"

"Hey, I've got an idea," Cass said suddenly. "Something that might make everyone happy."

"What?" Bryn's voice sounded flat.

"We said we wanted prom to be different this year, right?"

"Yeah. And a fund-raiser is different."

"But what if we opened prom up to everyone?"

"Everyone?"

"Yeah. All the classes would be welcome."

"Oh . . . I don't know . . ."

"We want to make lots of money for Sofia, don't we?" Cassidy remembered the numbers she'd been playing with this afternoon. "If it was open to everyone, we'd probably make a lot more money. Besides that, it might be good for school spirit. Everyone behind the same thing. And it would give the guys—especially guys like Lane—one less thing to argue about."

"Hmm . . . maybe."

"So think about it, okay?" Cass went back to the kitchen. "I gotta go help my mom with dinner, but just think about it, Bryn. It could be pretty cool. An all-inclusive prom."

Bryn agreed to consider this suggestion and, feeling a bit more hopeful, Cassidy hung up. Really, what did they have to lose by opening up the prom to everyone?

Although Devon chose not to be on the prom committee, she was still strongly in support of having prom. And whenever she heard classmates arguing over it, which was happening more and more, she freely stepped in. Devon had no problem expressing her rather loud opinions.

"Prom is a time-honored tradition," she hotly told a couple of guys in her fitness training class. "If you get rid of prom, what's next on your hit list? Graduation ceremonies? And what about sports? Want to get rid of football games and lacrosse matches? And what about band concerts and school plays? You want to nix those too? Maybe you should just strip everything extra out of school. Just like in the good old days," she was quoting Grandma Betty now. "Stick to reading, writing, and arithmetic." She rolled her eyes as she got onto the stair stepper.

Fortunately this shut the guys up. At least temporarily, anyway. But as she did her workout, she was irked at the males in this school. It was like they'd been brainwashed. First by Mr. Worthington with his "boys must be gentlemen" speech at the beginning of the school year and more recently by that silly youth pastor. She'd never seen such thickheaded and stubborn guys. Very childish.

"Something's got to be done," she told her DG friends as they gathered at Costello's for an "emergency" protect-the-prom meeting on Saturday morning. "The guys in this school are not backing down from their I-hate-prom campaign."

"If anything, they've gotten stronger," Emma told them. "Some of the girls have even gotten on their bandwagon."

"I really thought that when we opened prom up to all the classes, it would help," Cassidy said.

"I think it has helped," Bryn told her. "Without the freshman and sophomore girls' support, we'd be sunk by now. Unfortunately, it might not be enough."

"Maybe it's just the end of an era," Abby said gently. "Time for prom to just lie down and quietly die."

"*No!*" Bryn and Devon both exclaimed.

"And what about the fund-raiser part?" Emma asked. "By the way, Felicia said to tell you guys hi. She went with her dad to the treatment center to visit her sister. She couldn't wait to tell Sofia the good news about prom being a fund-raiser for her."

"How can we take that away now?" Bryn demanded.

"So does that mean Sofia's still at the same treatment center?" Cassidy asked Emma.

"She is for now. Since they'd already started her on chemo before the insurance pulled the plug, they've worked it out for her to stay up there awhile."

"Back to my point," Bryn said. "How can we take that

away from Sofia? We have to fight to keep prom and to keep it a fund raiser."

"But the guys are ready to put it to a student-body vote next week," Cassidy reminded them. "It might be out of our hands."

"Then it's time to bring out the big guns," Bryn declared.

"Ooh, I like that," Devon teased. "Bryn's getting feisty."

"She's just been watching action movies with her dad again," Abby told them. "That always gets her fired up."

"Yeah, whatever." Bryn placed her palms on the table with a steely gleam in her blue eyes. "But I happen to have a plan. A plan that I think will work."

"Cool." Devon leaned forward with interest.

"Remember I told you guys about promposals?" Bryn began.

"Yeah." Devon nodded eagerly. "I remember."

"Huh?" Emma looked confused.

"You were probably down in LA," Cassidy told her. "Living the big life on the red carpet."

Bryn pointed at Cassidy's iPad. "Go to YouTube and do a search on promposals, okay?"

Cassidy went into search mode.

"A promposal is kind of like a wedding proposal," Bryn told Emma. "And a lot of guys are planning these really fun, extravagant ways to ask girls to proms."

"I found one." Cassidy set her iPad in the center of the table and soon they were all watching as a bunch of kids did what seemed like a spontaneous flash dance, but ended with the dancers holding up cards that said SHELBY, WILL YOU GO TO PROM WITH ME?

"Oh, that's sweet," Emma said. "Look, Shelby is actually crying."

They looked at a few more, commenting and critiquing on which ones they liked or didn't like.

"Those are hilarious," Abby said, "but how does it solve anything?"

"Yeah," Emma agreed. "I mean, if the guys want to cancel prom altogether, how are we supposed to get a wacky promposal out of them?"

Bryn slowly closed Cassidy's iPad. "Because I want to make promposals part of the fund-raiser."

"Huh?" Cassidy frowned.

"Yeah, I'm kinda lost too," Emma confessed.

"That's because you're forgetting something," Bryn said in a challenging tone. "Remember the Christmas ball?"

"Of course. But what does that have to do with this?" Abby demanded.

"How did we get the guys on board?"

"Oh, I get it." Devon nodded eagerly. "I know where you're going with that, Bryn. You want to turn promposals into some kind of a contest, don't you?"

"And why not?" Bryn made a sly smile. "We come up with a prize that's big enough to entice a guy to step out of his comfort zone, and voila! He's planning out a fabulous promposal."

"Brilliant!" Devon said.

"And that means he's going to prom," Abby concluded.

"Exactly." Bryn nodded eagerly. "The big question is, what kind of prize will it take to get our guys to make fools of themselves?"

"Do they really have to make fools of themselves?" Cassidy asked.

"Well, you gotta admit that it would feel risky to put yourself out there like that." Devon tapped Cass's iPad. "I mean, doing something that crazy and extreme in the hopes that the girl will accept your invitation. That takes guts."

"And a really big prize," Abby said glumly. "Which takes money . . . and we're trying to raise money. This is starting to feel impossible to me."

"We'll get someone to donate a prize," Bryn told them.

"What kind of prize?" Devon asked with interest.

"Something big." Bryn frowned. "I'm not really sure yet."

"Yeah, maybe you can get someone to donate a new pickup or SUV," Cassidy said sarcastically. "I'm sure that shouldn't be too difficult."

"People donate used cars sometimes," Abby told Bryn.

"A *used* car?" Bryn shook her head. "That doesn't seem like a very tempting prize."

"What if it was a hot-looking used car?" Devon suggested.

"That could be thousands of dollars," Cassidy pointed out. "Money that could be given directly to Sofia's medical treatment. Why give it away in a car?"

"I agree," Abby told them. "The prize cannot be that huge."

"Yeah." Bryn nodded. "You guys are probably right. But there's got to be something that a guy would want to win badly enough to make a promposal." She pointed at Devon. "And you're going to help me find it."

"I am?" Devon just shrugged. "Okay, sure. I am."

Bryn turned to Emma and Cass. "You two are going to start putting together a campaign—we've got to publicize the promposal contest in a big way. There's no time to waste. We need posters and an ad on the school website and announcements on the school's radio station and, well, whatever."

"What about me?" Abby asked. "Everyone got an assignment but me."

Bryn's brow creased. "Well, you hang with guys a lot . . . I mean, doing track and stuff. Find out what it is that a guy really wants—"

"I can tell you what a guy really wants." Devon gave them all a sly look. She knew that she was playing a role here, but it was a role she still liked to play sometimes. Maybe just for the shock value.

"Oh, Devon." Emma rolled her eyes.

"Yeah." Bryn gave Devon a warning look. "Tone it down, girlfriend."

"So back to my assignment?" Abby waited.

"Find out what might get a guy to consider doing a promposal," Bryn told Abby. "You know, like electronics, or sports tickets, or the hottest new game, or a cool bike, or snowboard . . . you know, guy stuff."

Abby looked slightly perplexed. "Seriously? I'm supposed to go around asking guys about stuff like that? Really?"

"I don't know *how* you do it." Bryn sounded slightly irritated. "Just do it, okay?"

After the meeting wound down, Bryn invited Devon to go with her to approach some of the local businesses. "I want to check the climate," she told Devon as they walked down Main Street. "To see which people might be open to making donations. Not just for the prize, but for prom too." She pulled a flyer out of her oversized bag and handed it to Devon. "We'll make our appeal and leave these behind."

As they walked, Devon studied the flyer. With a sweet photo of Sofia and a short description of the Northwood Academy Prom Fund-Raiser, it was fairly compelling. The idea of hitting up businesses for donations wasn't exactly something Devon felt comfortable with. However, she watched Bryn do it—seeing how Bryn introduced herself, shook the person's hand, just exuded confidence. It was like being in some kind of training camp.

Finally as they were going into the town's biggest sporting goods store, Bryn handed a flyer to Devon. "You do it this time."

Devon battled her nerves as she asked for the store manager. But when he came out, she imitated Bryn by introducing herself and firmly shaking his hand. Next she handed him the flyer, explaining how young Sofia Ruez was very ill but having a struggle to get the best medical treatment for her particular type of leukemia. "The students at Northwood Academy plan to donate all proceeds from this year's prom to Sofia's medical expenses. But in order to do this we need the help of some local sponsors. We're inviting grocers and restaurants to participate by donating food for the dinner, and the Party Place to donate decorations and, well, things like that." She paused to catch her breath. "Naturally, any merchandise donations will be tax deductible too." She smiled brightly at the middle-aged man.

"But this is a sporting goods store." He creased his brow and rested his hand on the seat of a shiny red mountain bike. "What would we possibly have to donate for your prom?"

Devon looked down at the expensive bike beneath his hand. "Well, the big goal of this fund-raiser is to get as many people as possible to attend prom. Unfortunately, the guys at our school are dragging their feet just as much as they're clinging to their wallets."

He laughed. "Not surprising."

"So we've come up with this plan," Bryn jumped in, explaining to him about the promposal contest and how they hoped it would motivate the guys to get on board. "Especially if there's a really good prize." Bryn stroked the handlebar.

"Wow, you girls really are clever," he told them. "Maybe you should major in marketing after high school."

Bryn nodded. "That's not a bad idea."

"So you're thinking I should donate this bike for your 'promposal' prize?"

"Would you?" Devon stared at him with wide eyes.

He looked down at the bike then back at the girls. "Tell you what, I'll think about it. And I'll run it by the big boss. Maybe we can work out a deal. Our prize in exchange for some promotion at your school?"

"Absolutely!" Bryn eagerly agreed. "We'd be happy to do that."

"And it's really important that we know about this as soon as possible," Devon added. "We want to put pictures of the prize out there for everyone to see. In posters and on the website and, well, just everywhere."

"Yeah," Bryn added. "It's such a pretty bike. It'll look cool on posters."

"I see there are phone numbers here." He pointed to the flyer. "And you've listed your school advisor too. That's all good." He grinned at them. "I like you girls. And I like your gumption. Mostly I like that you're putting yourselves out there to help your friend's little sister." He shook both their hands again. "We'll see what we can do, okay?"

"Okay," they both said simultaneously.

"I'll try to get an answer to you by early next week."

Bryn and Devon thanked him, and as they exited the store, Devon felt a strange lightness in her feet.

"That was really fun," she told Bryn once they were outside. "I was kinda scared at first, but then I just started talking and it was really pretty cool."

"You were great," Bryn told her.

"I just tried to imitate you."

"Yeah, but that was quick thinking to suggest the bike for a prize."

"He seemed to really like the idea of free advertising."

"Yeah. I think he might actually give us that bike too."

"Did you see the price of it?" Devon wouldn't admit this to Bryn, but her mom had paid just a little more than that for a used car last year. Not a very good car, but at least it ran.

"I know!" Bryn nodded. "I actually had no idea a bike could cost that much."

"Do you think the bike would motivate guys to do promposals?"

"I'm sure it would motivate some of them. The stubborn tightwads."

"Hey, I have another idea," Devon said suddenly. "What if part of the promposal prize was to get a pair of free tickets to the prom too? That's one way to keep them from complaining about the cost. We tell them that everyone has a chance to win their tickets for free—if they come up with the best promposal."

"Excellent!" Bryn reached up to slap palms with Devon. "Now let's just hope we get that bike."

As Bryn drove them home, Devon checked her phone to see that Cassidy had left her a text message inviting her to youth group again. Devon's first impulse was to text back—*no thanks*. But there was something in her that was still curious . . . something that was nagging her to go again. And she was curious about Sam too. Something about what she'd said last week had sort of stuck with Devon. Maybe it was because of the similarities of their stories.

"Cassidy is nagging me to go to youth group with her." Devon tried to sound uninterested, just to see how Bryn would react.

"Uh-huh." Bryn stopped for a light.

"Do you ever go to youth group?"

"Yeah. Abby and I go to the one at our church. I mean, not all the time, but sometimes . . . Anyway, we used to. It's a pretty small group. Nothing like the one at Cassidy and Emma's church. Sometimes I wish I went to their church just so I could go to their youth group."

"Really?" Without thinking too hard, Devon keyed in her answer. *OK*. Even as she hit Send, she questioned herself. Still, it wasn't like she was making some big kind of lifetime commitment here. She was simply curious, that was all. Besides, there were boys there. And the youth pastor guy had promised that the guys and girls wouldn't be breaking into separate groups tonight. What could it hurt to go again?

Emma chewed on the end of her paintbrush as she studied the acrylic painting she'd spent most of the afternoon working on. It was her first attempt at Impressionism—trying to capture light and color in the form of a bouquet of spring wildflowers that she'd gathered on her way home from the DG meeting earlier today. It had seemed like a good idea at the time, but right now it was looking pretty messy. Fortunately the acrylic paints dried quickly and she could layer on more colors later if necessary.

"Hey, Em, what's up?" Cassidy said from behind her.

Emma jumped in surprise. "Thanks for scaring me half to death."

"Sorry. I knocked on the front door and no one answered."

"Mom's out with her girlfriends tonight, showing off her pictures of the LA trip."

"I thought you wanted a ride to youth group tonight."

Emma looked at her alarm clock by her bed. "Kinda early, aren't you?"

"We have to pick up Devon too." Cassidy peered curiously at the painting. "That's, uh, interesting . . . What is it?"

Emma rolled her eyes as she pointed her paintbrush toward the mason jar of wildflowers. "*That.*"

"Oh, yeah, I guess I can see it." Cassidy frowned at Emma. "But your paintings are usually, uh, a lot better than this. No offense."

"It's supposed to be Impressionism."

"Uh-huh . . . ?"

"Devon told me that she likes Impressionism—or at least she likes Vincent van Gogh. And it's her birthday next week. I wanted to make a painting for her."

"Well, that's nice." Cassidy still looked unconvinced. "I hope she likes it. But if you ever make me a birthday painting, just paint it normal, okay?"

Emma laughed. "It's a deal."

"What day is her birthday?"

"Wednesday."

"Well, we should tell Jarrod. You know how he likes to get everyone to sing his goofy Happy Birthday song."

"Yeah, that should embarrass her nicely." Emma looked more closely at Cassidy now. Her long dark-brown hair was all smooth and sleek, and she was wearing her best jeans and boots, topped with a pretty green pullover that actually showed off her curves. She even had on earrings. "You look really nice, Cass. Any reason to get all spiffed up?"

Cassidy shrugged like it was no big deal. "I just felt like it. I mean, last week, I went to youth group looking like a slob—or according to Devon, Pippi Longstocking." She told Emma about her messy braids and black rubber garden boots. "Anyway, I got to thinking about how the guys are all anti-prom right now . . . and Lane will probably be there tonight and I thought, hey, why not put my best foot forward." She made a sheepish grin. "I'm sure Devon and Bryn would approve."

"I'm sure they would." Emma looked down at her own paint-smeared shirt and jeans. "Maybe I should up my game a little too."

"Well, you have time." Cassidy sat down on Emma's bed. "We don't need to get Devon for about twenty minutes."

As Emma dressed, she told Cassidy about Felicia's latest phone call. "She's spending the night in Sofia's room at the pediatric center tonight. The room's set up with an extra bed so that a family member can stay over. I guess Felicia's mom's worn out after being there all week. She'll stay in the hotel with Felicia's dad."

"It must be hard. So how's Sofia doing?"

"Sounds like she's starting to feel pretty sick from the chemotherapy treatments." Emma tugged on a clean pair of jeans. "Felicia says it's like having a really bad case of the flu."

"Has her hair fallen out?"

"Felicia didn't mention it." Emma ran her fingers through her own short haircut, fluffing it up a little. Then she turned to face Cassidy. "Felicia said that Sofia's going to need a bone marrow transplant. The Ruezes are encouraging everyone in their family to register to be donors."

"I wonder if we could register too," Cassidy said.

"I asked Felicia the same thing. She says you have to be eighteen."

"Oh . . ."

"But she said we could get the word out."

"Maybe we could get something in the school paper, just to make kids aware, you know, in case their parents or other adults might be willing to register," Cassidy suggested.

"You're a good writer," Emma pointed out. "Maybe you could tackle that."

"Yeah, definitely." Cass nodded. "I'll ask Felicia for more information next week. Maybe it could even run in the local newspaper. And our church's newsletter too."

"Good ideas." Emma slid her feet into her shoes. "Ready!"

As they drove to Emma's grandmother's house, Emma thanked Cassidy for enticing Devon to go to youth group last week. "She'd sounded so lost and desperate in her texts to me," Emma told her. "I could tell it was her way of reaching out."

"I was actually pretty surprised that she agreed to go," Cassidy admitted.

"Devon tries to act like she's got it all together, like she's really tough. But underneath all that, I know she's just a scared, lonely girl. And even though she drives me crazy sometimes, I really do care about her."

"Yeah. Me too." Cassidy told Emma about the new youth leader. "At first I was a little suspicious—I mean, Sam is so pretty, I just thought she might end up being an airhead, you know?"

"That's kind of judgmental."

Cass laughed. "Tell me about it."

"But you like her?"

"I really do. And I think Devon liked her too. Oh, she didn't say anything to that effect, but I saw her watching Sam. And when we drove home, she didn't say anything negative about her. That's when I figured she probably did like her. Otherwise she would've dissed her."

Emma chuckled. "Good observation."

"See, I've been paying attention." Cassidy pulled her car into Emma's grandma's driveway, giving a quick beep on her horn.

"I'll run in and get her," Emma offered. "And say hi to my grandma."

Inside the house, Emma hugged her grandma then glanced around for Devon. "Is she in her room?"

"Here I am." Devon came into the kitchen.

"Hey . . . ," Emma said slowly, taking in Devon's slightly unusual outfit—at least for Devon. She had on a baggy plaid flannel shirt, a holey pair of jeans, and a shabby pair of Converse canvas shoes. Not only that, but her makeup looked very natural and her thick auburn hair was pulled back in a ponytail. "Are you, uh, ready?"

"Yep." Devon grinned at Grandma. "See ya later."

Emma kissed Grandma's cheek and, trying not to stare at Devon, headed out the door.

As they walked to the car, Emma was tempted to question Devon about her appearance, but she knew that could turn out badly. Instead, she told Devon that she'd talked to Felicia this afternoon.

"How's she doing?" Devon asked after they were in the car.

Emma filled her in, exchanging glances with Cassidy, who looked just as bewildered as Emma felt.

"Looks like you were working in the garden today," Cassidy said to Devon as she turned into the church parking lot.

"Really?" Devon made a nervous-sounding giggle. "Well, I realized that your youth group was a pretty casual place. So why bother to fix up?"

"Yeah . . . right . . ." Cassidy sounded a bit uncertain as she parked her car. "The most important thing is to show up."

"That's right," Emma agreed as they got out. "Besides, I think you look fabulous, Devon."

"Really?" Devon peered suspiciously at her.

"Absolutely." Emma flipped Devon's ponytail. "It's a nice look. Fresh and fun and down-to-earth." And Emma was being totally honest. She actually preferred this over the way Devon usually looked—too much makeup, too-tight clothes, and just too flashy. Hopefully this was a sample of things to come.

As they went into the youth group room, Emma's eyes scanned the crowd until she spotted Isaac. Then, as she'd been doing lately, she quickly looked the other way—acting nonchalant and as if she hadn't seen him. Oh, she knew it was a bit childish, but this recent debate over the prom had hurt her feelings slightly. It wasn't anything she planned to admit to anyone, but it was a fact.

Emma's friendship with Isaac had been moving forward nicely—ever since their first date last fall. She never would've gone so far as to call him her boyfriend. Not out loud, anyway. But she felt like they had an understanding. And, unless she'd imagined it, he had hinted about taking her to prom this year.

But then he'd jumped on the guys' anti-prom bandwagon and that's when Emma had taken a step back. For the past few days, she had been acting fairly chilly toward him. And, as much as she liked him, she was aggravated at him too.

Emma spotted Jarrod coming in through a back door with his guitar in hand. "I'll go tell Jarrod our little idea," she whispered to Cass. "For Devon."

Cass's eyes lit up. "Oh, yeah."

Emma popped up to the front area and quickly relayed to Jarrod about Devon's upcoming birthday. "She's not a regular youth group girl," she explained. "But she was here last week—and came again tonight."

"Cool." He nodded with a twinkle in his eye. "We'll be sure to make her feel welcome tonight."

"Thanks."

"Hey, how was the big red carpet?" he asked suddenly. "The kids were showing me some photos last week. Was it a blast?"

"Yeah. It was amazing." As she was filling him in on some of the celebs she'd spotted, Isaac joined them. Probably because of Isaac's presence, Emma proceeded to color the red carpet a little more brightly.

"Very cool." Jarrod waved across the room. "Hey, if you two will excuse me, there's a guy I need to talk to."

And suddenly it was just Isaac and Emma, standing by themselves up front. Emma folded her arms across her midsection, gazing evenly at Isaac—and wishing he didn't look so doggone cute with his shaggy sandy hair and clear blue eyes. She vaguely wondered if she was a good enough artist to do a decent portrait of him, then mentally slapped herself. *Stop it!*

"So Em, how's it going?" he said a bit cautiously.

"Just great." She gave him an overly bright smile.

"I haven't seen much of you since your LA trip. I got to thinking that maybe you've turned into something of a celebrity yourself—too good to talk to the common people." He made a lopsided smile.

"Seriously?" She glared at him. "You thought that?"

"Well, not seriously." His smile faded slightly. "But you sure seem standoffish lately. Did I do something to offend you?"

She felt herself bristling as she shrugged.

"Come on, Em. I thought we were . . . uh . . . *friends*."

"Yeah, I thought so too." She forced another smile.

"Then why are you freezing me out?"

She considered her words. She wanted to be honest with him, and yet . . . "Okay, here's the deal, Isaac. When you got behind the whole anti-prom thing, well, it felt kinda like a slap in the face. Ya know?"

He rubbed his chin like he was thinking hard. "So going to prom means *that much* to you?"

She tilted her head to one side. "To be honest, I didn't think that it did . . . I mean, *before*. But maybe it's just feeling like you don't like me well enough to ask me." She shrugged uneasily. "Well, that kinda hurts."

Isaac looked genuinely sorry. "That's not how I feel at all."

"Really?"

And now he opened his arms and enveloped her in a big, warm hug. "I really like you, Emma," he said quietly.

When they stepped away, she felt slightly embarrassed, but happy too. "I guess I shouldn't be taking it so seriously," she admitted. "But Felicia is a very good friend, and we really do want to make money to help her sister. I guess that's made prom seem even more important."

"Yeah . . . I get that. And I can't speak for all the guys, but I care about Felicia's sister too. I want to do whatever we can to help her."

"You do?"

"Absolutely. Maybe it's time we all got on the same page. Don't you think?"

Before she could respond, Jarrod and the other musicians were starting to play, and everyone was starting to take their seats.

"Can I sit with you?" Isaac asked.

She nodded with a happy grin. Of course, as she sat with

Isaac up in the front row, she could tell that Cassidy and Devon were watching. And judging by Cassidy's frown, she probably thought Emma had crossed enemy lines. But, really, the guys weren't their enemies just because they didn't agree. Isaac was right. It was about time for everyone to get on the same page.

You were a really good sport tonight," Cassidy told Devon as she drove them home from youth group. "I thought you were about to throw a hissy fit when Jarrod put that goofy birthday crown on your head."

"Me too," Emma confessed. "And I figured you'd probably tear into me since I was the one who told him about your birthday."

"Yeah, I was getting ready to kill someone . . . at first anyway." Devon chuckled in the backseat. "But once everyone started singing that crazy birthday song, well, it wasn't too bad."

"And you looked very cute up there," Emma assured her.

"Really?"

"Yeah. I got a couple of photos to prove it."

"Cool. Send them."

"What did you guys think of Jarrod's talk tonight?" Cassidy asked the question with caution. "I mean, it gave me something to think about, you know?" It wasn't that she wanted to put them on the spot, but she was curious to hear Devon's response—especially since it was her second time in a row to come to youth group. Was it possible that Devon was giving these messages some serious consideration? But as the car got quiet Cassidy felt uneasy. Maybe she shouldn't have asked. Was she being intrusive, too pushy?

"I thought it was a good challenge for everyone," Emma eventually said. "It's sort of easy to misjudge people. I know I should probably work on that."

"Yeah," Cassidy agreed. "Me too. You guys know how judgmental I can be sometimes. It's so easy to assume the worst about someone—especially when you don't really know them."

"Or if you find them particularly irritating," Emma added.

"Or just plain don't like them." Cassidy stopped at the light.

"I really liked what Jarrod said about how the people who are hurting the worst are usually the ones to do the worst hurting," Emma continued. "To be honest, that's not something I normally think about when someone hurts my feelings."

"Yeah," Cassidy agreed. "And I don't usually think about what it feels like to be in someone else's shoes—especially if I don't like how they're treating me."

The car got quiet and Cassidy considered pressing Devon for her opinion, but then decided not to. Better to just pray for her. Patience wasn't Cassidy's strong suit, but she was learning.

"Well, Jarrod's talk did give me some things to think about too," Devon quietly told them. "I guess that's a good thing."

"Yeah." Cassidy nodded eagerly. "That is good."

"Now, not to change the subject," Devon said suddenly, "but I have to tell you guys about what Bryn and I did today." Without missing a beat, she launched into the story of how she and Bryn went around soliciting donations from businesses. "At first I was like, no way am I going to do this—I mean, just walk into a store and ask the manager to hand over some merchandise—*for free*? But I watched how Bryn handled it, and finally when she said it was my turn, I just imitated her—kinda like I was playing a dramatic role. And it was actually pretty fun."

"Interesting," Emma said. "I wish I could've seen that."

Devon told them about how they might get an expensive bike donated for the promposal prize. "The manager dude promised to let us know soon."

"Awesome," Cassidy said.

"Too bad girls can't do promposals," Emma said with a longing tone. "I'd love to win a new bike."

"Who said girls can't?" Cassidy asked.

"Really?" Emma sounded doubtful.

"Why not?"

"But the promposal contest is supposed to get *guys* interested," Devon protested. "You know, to get prom attendance up."

"So . . . ?" Cassidy turned onto Devon's street.

"So . . . what if girls enter the contest and come up with great promposals, but the guys refuse to go?" Devon challenged.

"Good point," Emma conceded. "I guess the contest should be only for guys."

"That seems sexist to me," Cassidy told them. "Discriminatory."

"I gotta agree," Emma said. "And not just because I'd love to win a bike."

"But it could ruin everything," Devon argued. "I mean, think about it. What if Emma did this fabulous promposal, but then Isaac said no thanks? Where would we be?"

"Why would Isaac say no?" Emma asked.

"Because you hurt his male pride?" Devon offered.

"Hmm." Emma sounded stumped.

"I know what we do," Cassidy declared. "One of the conditions to enter the promposal contest will be that the promposal must result in a couple attending prom. Otherwise, the promposal is ineligible."

"Yes," Emma agreed. "That makes sense."

"I don't know . . . but I guess it could work." Devon sounded a bit reluctant.

"It seems more fair." Cassidy stopped to let Devon out. "I mean, think about it, a bunch of girls went to prom last year—*without* guys. The contest shouldn't exclude them just because they're girls. Whoever wants to support prom should be able to enter the promposal contest."

"I agree," Emma declared.

"Well, it's a good thing you guys are both on prom committee." Devon got out of the car. "Good luck working out all these details with Bryn and the others." She laughed, then politely thanked Cassidy for the ride and ran up to the house.

"I think something's going on with Devon," Emma said quietly as Cassidy backed out of the driveway.

"Something good?"

"I hope so." Emma sighed. "I mean, she seems different. In a positive way."

"You said her birthday's on Wednesday?" Cassidy drove toward Emma's house.

"Yeah. That reminds me, I better send her the photos I took tonight. She really was a good sport, wasn't she?"

"I think she likes the attention."

"Yeah, well, that's nothing new." Emma finished sending the pics, then put her phone away. "And if you think about her family and stuff—and combine that with what Jarrod said tonight—it all sort of makes sense."

"I know what you mean." Cassidy nodded. "Hey, what if we did something special for her birthday? She's had a pretty rough year. All that stuff with her mom . . . then moving in with your grandma. Do you think Devon would like a little surprise party? Maybe just invite the DG?"

"That's a great idea. Devon loves attention. And I doubt her mom will do anything for her. But I'm sure I could get my grandma to throw a cake together. She loves to bake."

By the time Cassidy dropped Emma off, they'd managed to put together a surprise party plan. If anyone had told Cassidy last fall that she'd be into something like this now, she would've thought they were crazy. Especially considering how she used to really dislike Devon. Funny how people could change . . . if you gave them time.

• • ● • •

Cassidy and Emma had already heard the good news, but everyone else on the prom committee got to hear it on Tuesday after school. Bryn called the meeting to order and immediately made the announcement.

"Not only has Richardson's Sporting Goods donated a very cool mountain bike, they've thrown in some other items too." Bryn held up the letter the store had faxed to the school this morning. "Including a backpack, sleeping bag, and some other cool-looking camp stuff."

"It will make a really enticing prize," Cassidy told them. "If we got some photos of the bike and these items, we could probably put together a fairly cool poster." She pointed at Emma. "You're a good photographer. Maybe you should make a stab at it."

"I could probably do it for my graphic design project," Emma said.

"Great idea," Bryn told her. "I appoint Emma to handle that." She went over the other prom donations that they'd managed to solicit from other businesses—all sorts of things, from ten pounds of mixed nuts to a fake tree. "But we still need more." Bryn handed a printout to the committee members. "I've made a list of stuff we can still use. We'll break down this list between us. And then I want everyone to start scouting more donations."

"Why does everything have to be donated?" Amanda Norton asked with what sounded like irritation. Amanda had just joined prom committee and Cassidy wasn't sure if that was a good thing or not. Sometimes Amanda seemed genuinely helpful. But sometimes she just made things more difficult. And Abby felt certain that Amanda's motives had more to do with being crowned prom queen than wanting to help. However, Cassidy was trying to keep Jarrod's recent sermon in mind. Don't judge . . . walk in their shoes . . . be ruled by love.

"Because every dollar we save goes directly to Sofia Ruez," Bryn explained to Amanda. "Every item that's donated—not purchased—means more profits, and whatever we end up with gets doubled when the Hartford Foundation gifts their matching funds."

"Oh . . ." Amanda just nodded. "Okay, I get that."

"What about the prom location?" Mazie Tucker asked. "Have you gotten anyone to donate that yet?"

"I'm working on it. But I must admit that it's been tricky." Bryn sighed. "The venue that the school already reserved, the Renaldo, refuses to donate their ballroom. The best they can do is a small discount."

"Stingy Renaldo," Cassidy said. "I'll remind my parents to stop eating at their restaurant."

Some of the others laughed, agreeing to boycott the hotel too.

"And the other hotels are already booked for our prom night," Bryn explained.

"Everything is booked?" Amanda asked.

"So far it is. From mid-April on out I haven't found a thing." Bryn sighed.

"Why can't we have prom right here in our school?" Cassidy asked. "In the gym."

Naturally, this resulted in a lot of protests and complaints, not to mention just plain whining. Cassidy was about to tell them that they were a bunch of babies, but decided that wouldn't help matters. "But what if we really decorated the gym up big time?" she suggested. "If we made it look like something completely different than a gym. Maybe go with a theme."

This was followed by more groaning, along with some snide comments.

"But just think of the money we'd save," she pressed. "Money that could go to Sofia." She picked up one of the

Sofia posters now, holding it up so that they could all look into the little girl's big brown eyes.

"We could probably make the gym work," Emma said cautiously. "It would take a lot of work to make it look, uh, different. But it could probably be done."

"Prom in the gym?" Amanda sounded scandalized. "You gotta be kidding!" She pointed at Bryn. "Seriously, you're saying out of all the hotels in town, there's not one ballroom available for us?"

"Not for free." Bryn folded her arms in front of her. "Not on our date anyway."

"Well, how about a different date?" Amanda said. "A later date perhaps?"

Bryn picked up her notes. "The next date that we can get—I mean, one that's donated for free—isn't until late May. And it's not a very nice venue either." She pointed to her paper. "Or else there's this night at Le Chateau, but it's—"

"*Le Chateau?*" Amanda exclaimed. "They've offered us their ballroom for free?"

"Le Chateau is gorgeous," Mazie said.

"Yeah," Cassidy agreed. "I went to a wedding there. It's really beautiful."

"Yes, I know," Bryn said crisply. "The problem with Le Chateau is the date they've offered."

"When is it?" Emma asked.

"The Saturday right after spring break," Bryn told them. "And like I told the manager at Le Chateau, that's just too soon."

"Who says it's too soon?" Cassidy demanded.

"I say it's too soon," Bryn replied.

"Why?" Emma asked. "That's, like, three weeks off, isn't it?"

"But we're barely off the ground," Bryn told her. "So far

we haven't sold a single ticket. I told you guys already that planning prom is a lot like planning a wedding. You do not rush it."

"But if Le Chateau gives us their ballroom for free," Cassidy argued, "wouldn't that be worth rushing for?"

"But there's so much to do. Not just for prom, but we all have to get our dresses and everything," Bryn said. "It takes time."

Cassidy held up her iPad to where she'd pulled up a calendar. "But we actually have three and a half weeks. See. That's plenty of time to find a dress and shoes."

"And we already got the promposal prize," Emma reminded them. "I'll get those posters designed and up in just a couple of days. I might even work on it at home tonight. We can do this, Bryn. I know we can."

Amanda looked doubtful. "I'm inclined to agree with Bryn on this. Seriously, three and a half weeks? And one of them is spring break? It feels too rushed to me."

"You want to lose out on Le Chateau?" Cassidy challenged. "A beautiful venue like that, and it's totally free? Do you guys really need those extra weeks? Just to pick out your dress and shoes?" She pointed at Bryn. "You're saying you would give up Le Chateau just to gain a few weeks of shopping time?"

"Well, no . . . but I—"

"No buts," Emma declared. "I move we put this to a vote."

"I second the motion," Cassidy said quickly.

Finally, after a bit more arguing and a couple of heartfelt reminders that the prom fund-raiser was meant to benefit Sofia Ruez, Emma's motion was put to a vote. Scheduling prom a few weeks earlier than planned, at the lovely Le Chateau, won with better than a two-thirds majority. And when it was said and done, Cassidy felt surprisingly victorious over the results. Interesting, since she had never been much into prom in the first place. But the idea of helping little Sofia was motivating. And it seemed a worthwhile reason to hold prom a few weeks earlier than some people felt was convenient.

Cassidy felt a tiny bit bad when, walking to their locker bay, Bryn continued to lament that there wasn't sufficient time to find the right dress, acting like she truly believed that prom was the next best thing to a wedding. But Cass also felt fairly certain that her fashionista friend would show up at prom dressed to the nines. Yet one big question remained—would the guys get on board with prom? What if no one bought tickets?

Abby tried to be understanding to Bryn as they got into Bryn's car. After all, Bryn had patiently waited for Abby to finish track practice, just to give her a ride home. Never mind that Abby had been hoping Kent might offer a ride. But it was obvious that Bryn's nose was out of joint about something related to prom. And the more Abby listened, the muddier it seemed to get.

"So let me get this clear," Abby said finally. "You're bummed because prom's going to be held at Le Chateau?"

"No, I'm glad it'll be at Le Chateau. That's a beautiful venue. They have the best ballroom in town, and their chandeliers are from France. I'm upset that we have to reschedule prom earlier just to get Le Chateau. What I'm trying to tell you is that our prom is just a little over three weeks off now! Can you believe it?"

"What's wrong with that?"

"Are you kidding? It's horrible news. Before, we had over six weeks to get ready. Now it's more like three."

"Three weeks sounds fine. And if you're excited about prom, wouldn't you be glad that it's coming quicker? Kinda like Christmas when we were kids?"

"No, it's not like that at all. Okay, sure it would be just fine if you were ready. Like if you already found the perfect gown and shoes and accessories and everything. And if you'd made your hair appointment, a mani-pedi appointment, and maybe a spray tan, and if your flowers were ordered and you'd—"

"Seriously? You really believe everyone who goes to prom will do all of that, Bryn? Because I assure you, I won't."

"Well, duh." Bryn laughed. "Lucky for you, you don't *need* a spray tan."

"Very funny."

"And, oh yeah, I left out one little detail. *A date.*"

"Oh . . ." Abby smoothed her hair. The damp spring air had made it frizz up. Although just this afternoon, while waiting for the guys to finish up in the high-jump pit, Kent had told her he liked it that way.

"Aren't you listening to me?" Bryn demanded.

"Sorry." Abby smiled to herself. "Guess I was spacing a little."

"I was just saying that this means everyone has to get über-busy—we've got to work fast. That's why I'm calling an emergency DG meeting for tomorrow evening."

"But I thought we were having that surprise party for Devon tomorrow night."

"We are, but it will have to be part surprise party and part DG meeting. Because we've got to get this thing with the guys off center. We need them to step up. I mean, it's not impossible to shop for a dress without a date lined up, but I personally think it's easier to do it the other way."

Abby laughed. "I've seen you do it the other way."

"Maybe so, but I'd like to do it right for prom."

"So who are you hoping will ask you?" Abby glanced at Bryn's profile. Even with her forehead creased and her mouth puckered up, Bryn was still very pretty. You'd think she'd have an easy time getting dates, although this past year had proved otherwise.

"I honestly don't know."

"Not Jason, I hope."

"No, definitely not Jason, although for a guy who acts like he's boycotting prom, he's dropped a couple of hints my way. At least I think they were hints." She sighed. "Don't tell anyone, but I've been wondering about Lane. I have this funny feeling that he'd like to ask me."

"Lane?" Abby tried not to sound too distressed. She knew that Cassidy was hoping for Lane to ask her. In fact, Cassidy had even suggested that she might ask him first. "What makes you think Lane might ask you?"

"For starters, he's been pretty friendly lately. And just today he asked me what we were doing in response to the guys' boycott efforts."

"Maybe he was just being congenial. Lane's a nice guy. He talks to lots of people. Doesn't mean he's going to ask them out."

"I don't know . . . I think there's more to it." Bryn stopped for the red light. "And you have to admit, he's good-looking. I mean, sure, he's not as hot as Jason, but he's a lot nicer. I think I've reached the point in life where I'd take a good guy over a hot guy. You know what I mean?" She looked earnestly at Abby.

"Yeah. Fortunately, Kent is both." Abby laughed.

"Unfortunately, we're not all as lucky as you." Bryn rolled her eyes.

Abby still wasn't ready to drop the Lane question yet. "But what about Cassidy?" she said gently. "I thought she still liked Lane . . ."

"Really?" Bryn frowned as she pulled into the intersection. "It's so hard to tell with her. She runs hot and cold. I mean, she acts kind of like she could take him or leave him, you know? I figured if she was going to leave him, maybe I'd just scoop him up."

"Meaning you're going to ask him?" Abby tried to disguise her concern.

Bryn just shrugged, but her expression suggested she was considering this.

"But I thought we all agreed that we were going to wait, to step back and let the guys do the asking this time."

"That seemed like a good idea back when we thought we had more time. But with less than four weeks and one of them being spring break—and we really must have our dates nailed down *before* spring break—well, the rules might have to change."

"So when does the promposal contest officially begin?"

"Cass took Emma over to the sporting goods store to take some photos of the bike and other prizes, and Emma promised to start working on the poster tonight. It might be a rush job, but our hope is to start getting posters up by the end of the week. In the meantime, Cass is writing something for the school website and we prepared announcements to start playing on the school radio station. Everyone should pretty much know by the end of the day tomorrow."

"So we could start seeing promposals any day now?" Suddenly Abby was toying with the idea of springing a promposal on Kent this week. She wondered what he'd say. Maybe she could have a pizza delivered to him at the end of track practice. That would be sure to score points since everyone was always famished by then. She could glue a note into the top of the pizza box, inviting him to prom. Maybe she could make up some kind of pizza pun.

"Earth to Abby." Bryn's voice was laced with irritation.

"Huh?" Abby turned to look at her. "Did you say something?"

"I was just telling you what the theme for prom is going to be, but you were totally spaced out again."

"Sorry."

"What's on your mind anyway? Some big test? The track meet? College applications?"

"Actually, I was just imagining doing a promposal for Kent."

"Seriously?" Bryn laughed. "You'd really do that? I thought you were pretty sure that Kent was going to ask you."

"He's hinted . . . but you never know. And, hey, I agree with Emma, I wouldn't mind winning a bike myself. Why let the guys have all the fun?"

"Then you'd have to come up with a really good promposal," Bryn pointed out. "Anything particular in mind?"

"Not really. I was thinking a pizza delivery. Maybe I could have them spell out PROM in pepperoni. With a question mark."

Bryn laughed. "That's not bad, but I don't think it'll win you anything."

"Probably not. Maybe I better noodle on this some more."

"Anyway, I was telling you that Emma suggested a theme for prom. The red carpet. Well, we all know where that's coming from. And it's not a bad idea really, but it's just so cliché, you know? I pointed out that probably half the proms in this country use the red carpet for their theme. But then Mazie Tucker jumps in and starts going on about a Hawaiian prom with grass skirts and coconuts. And then this other girl suggests a DIY prom."

"DIY?"

"Do it yourself." Bryn groaned.

"Huh?"

"This whack-a-doodle girl starts talking about making prom dresses out of duct tape and aluminum foil and Kleenex boxes and garden hoses. And Emma was actually getting into it. Naturally, because it would be cheap. Anyway, as you can imagine, I got pretty worried. A dress out of garden hoses, can you imagine?"

"Might be interesting. Maybe we could have a contest for most creative DIY dress."

"Oh, Abby, I didn't expect you to go to the dark side."

Abby laughed. "So, let me guess, you put the kibosh on the garden hose gowns and climbed onto the red carpet bandwagon?"

"Absolutely. Besides, a red carpet theme means that shopping is pretty much wide open. We can have full-length gowns or cocktail dresses or whatever suits our fancy. I mean, we all watched the Oscars' red carpet when Emma and Felicia were down there. Anything goes . . . as long as it's elegant."

"At least more elegant than garden hoses."

"Right."

• ••• •

At dinner that night, Abby broached the prom topic with her parents. She knew that her dad would be opposed to her going to prom. He was opposed to pretty much anything involving boys and bare shoulders. But she felt certain that she could get Mom on her side. She started the conversation by telling them about the girl who wanted DIY dresses. Naturally, both her parents thought this was funny.

"And it's a great idea," Dad said. "Forcing kids to use their creativity instead of their parents' pockets."

"Well, that might be true, but the committee has decided to go with the red carpet for prom," Abby informed them. She told them about how prom was meant to be another fund-raiser, explaining about Felicia's little sister.

"I really like how you kids are reaching out," Mom told her. "I love the idea of prom not just being about prom."

"It's a nice thought," Dad agreed. "But I doubt you can really raise much money for the Ruez girl. Do you have any idea what medical treatment costs these days?"

Mom frowned at him. "But every little bit helps."

Abby told them about the Hartfords' generous matching funds offer and how many donations were being sought for prom itself. "That should make a difference. They raised the price of prom tickets too. That should help."

Dad had his phone on calculator mode and, after asking her some quick questions, he was doing some fast figuring. "Let's be optimistic and say two hundred couples go." He started spewing out numbers based on potential ticket sales, and despite his gloomy predictions, Abby thought the numbers sounded pretty good.

"But do you realize that for every ticket purchased, the prom attendees are probably spending twice that much in preparation for the prom? And that's probably a conservative estimate."

"Well, I don't know about that."

"Think about this, Abby. If everyone decided to cancel prom and simply donate what they would've spent, that little Ruez girl could have . . ." He paused to calculate, then tossed out a number that was about three times higher than his first estimate.

"Wow." Abby sighed. "That's a lot of money. I mean, if it could happen like that—canceling prom and donating the money."

"But that's no fun." Mom scowled as she began to clear the table. "Kids need to have prom and girls need pretty dresses. It can't all just be about the money. Good grief."

Abby stood to help her mom. "I know," Abby conceded, "but I get what Dad's saying too. That's a lot of money. It could really help Sofia Ruez."

Mom put a hand on Abby's shoulder. "You kids are already helping Sofia, just by turning your prom into a fund-raiser."

"But maybe we can do more," Abby said as she carried the dishes into the kitchen.

As Abby loaded the dishwasher, she thought about what her dad had said about how much money the average couple would be laying down for one night. Certainly not all the couples, because not everyone was as committed to fashion as Bryn. But she also knew that most of the kids at their school were fairly comfortable. Their parents wouldn't think much of doling out the cash. Oh, sure, they'd complain—just like her dad would do—but in the end they would fork it over.

After she finished in the kitchen, Abby went online to do some research on the average costs of prom dresses and tuxedoes. To her surprise, she found lots of great resources that offered used designer gowns for very low prices and even some online rental gown sites—far more options than she'd thought were out there. By the time she started in on her homework, she had a plan in place.

She would call it the Prom Budget Challenge—aka the PBC. She wasn't sure of all the details, but somehow she would kick off a campaign to encourage classmates to consider ways they could save rather than spend money on prom. And the saved money would be donated into the Sofia fund.

Perhaps she'd create a blog where she'd list the websites she'd found. Or maybe work some kind of deal with the formal rental shop downtown. Perhaps some free advertising at school. But somehow she had to make the idea of spending less and giving more seem cool. Instead of kids going around bragging about how much they'd spent on prom, they could brag about how much money they saved—and donated toward a little girl's fight with leukemia.

Some might think it was a crazy idea, or perhaps not even worth the effort, but she was committed to carrying it through. She honestly thought it could pay off. Okay, maybe renting a gown wouldn't fly with someone like Bryn. But she felt certain that a lot of other students at Northwood would go for this. At the very least, it was worth a try.

By lunchtime on Wednesday, Bryn had already selected about a dozen prom dress possibilities that she was eager to show her friends. To this end, she had Cassidy's iPad in the center of the lunch table, and as soon as all members of the DG were present, she started to explain her plan.

"I realize that we don't all like the same kinds of gowns," she began, "and it's not like I think we have to be totally coordinated, but as you guys know, I'm the one who pays the most attention to fashion and I just think that since we hang together and we'll probably be at prom together, well, it might look better if our dresses went nicely with each other. You know, instead of clashing, or looking all out of place or weird."

"Oh, no." Cassidy let out a groan. "Here we go again."

"Really, Bryn, don't you think we're smart enough to pick out our own prom dresses?" Devon made an exasperated sigh.

"Yeah, instead of obsessing over prom dresses, maybe we should figure out how to get dates." Abby frowned.

"But this is important," Bryn protested. "Time's limited and there are fittings and alterations and—"

"I agree with Abby," Emma interrupted. "What point is there in getting a dress if you don't have a date?"

"We could always just go to prom together," Cassidy suggested. "All the DG girls renting a limo and—"

"No way!" Devon exclaimed. "I am not going to prom with a bunch of girls. That is so lame."

"I don't know." Abby shrugged. "Might be fun to be free to dance with all the guys."

"All the guys?" Devon frowned. "What if no guys go? So far, from what I've heard, no one's been asked to prom yet."

"No kidding." Emma held up her hands in a hopeless gesture. "I thought I'd get invited by now. But Isaac is being really stubborn about this. I pretty much came right out and told him on Saturday that I wanted him to ask me to prom. And he seemed genuinely sympathetic. But he hasn't mentioned it once since then. I honestly don't get it."

"It's because of the prom boycott petition," Felicia said. "I heard a couple guys talking about it in math. It's like they think since they signed the boycott, it would be hypocritical for them to ask a girl to prom."

"We really need one of the guys to step up and take one for the team," Abby declared.

"Yeah," Devon agreed. "How about Kent? You guys are almost a couple."

Abby rolled her eyes. "Calling us a couple is an exaggeration. But I honestly thought Kent would ask me to prom. And I've been hinting about it, but he's still dragging his heels."

"Yeah, yeah," Bryn said with impatience. "I know all about the guy problem and I agree we need to do something about it. But right now I wanted to talk about dresses." She pointed to a long pale-blue gown with gorgeous beadwork. "I really like this one," she began, "but it might be a little too princessy, you know? And it wouldn't look very good next to a dress like, say, this one." She pointed to a glittery purple cocktail-length dress. "Although I do think this is a great design and—"

Abby held up a hand to stop Bryn. "Hey, before we get too involved in dress decisions, I have an announcement to make."

Bryn frowned at Abby. "An announcement?"

Abby nodded. "And it has to do with prom dresses too."

"Oh?" Bryn smiled. Maybe Abby was on her side after all. "Okay, what is it, Abs?"

"I created a blog that will go live this afternoon," Abby told them. "It's called the PBC. That stands for Prom Budget Challenge."

"What's that?" Emma leaned forward with interest.

Abby started to explain the plan she'd cooked up. She wanted everyone to be really frugal while shopping for prom. Bryn thought it sounded ridiculous. "Instead of buying expensive gowns, girls can rent them or buy used or borrow—"

"You have got to be kidding!" Bryn stared at her best friend.

"I'm totally serious." Abby locked eyes with her. "My dad figured out how much money will be wasted on prom clothes that are only—"

"That's so like your dad," Bryn shot back at her. "Mr. *Tightwad*."

"He makes a very good point," Abby argued. "It's a one-night deal, and if you add up how much money everyone in this school will waste on stupid formal wear that they'll never use again, it's a pretty staggering figure." Abby pointed to Felicia. "And that money would be better spent on Sofia's cancer treatments."

"How does it work exactly?" Cassidy asked Abby.

"People will register on my blog. They'll put in the amount of money they expect to lay out for prom—kind of like a budget. Then we'll help them to find better deals for everything. And we'll keep track of the savings, and the cool part of the challenge is that they'll commit to donate their savings to the Sofia fund. So they end up getting what they need for prom and helping Sofia too."

"That's so sweet of you," Felicia told Abby.

"I love this idea," Emma chimed in. "Makes perfect sense to me."

"Well, I do *not* love it," Bryn declared. "I couldn't stand to wear a rented or borrowed gown. And I don't think you can make people do something they don't want to."

"Of course not," Abby agreed. "It's totally voluntary. Not everyone will want to be part of this. But it might appeal to some."

Bryn shoved Cassidy's iPad back at her. "Then I suppose it's pointless to show you guys the dresses I thought you might like. Never mind that I spent most of last night picking some good ones out."

"Why is it pointless?" Abby asked.

"Because it sounds like you all plan to show up in sackcloth and ashes." Bryn frowned at them. When had her friends turned into such party poopers? Wasn't prom supposed to be fun? Shopping for the perfect ensemble was just part of the fun . . . wasn't it?

"The websites I've listed on my blog have some really great-looking dresses," Abby told her.

"Don't forget the dresses we wore to the Christmas ball," Emma reminded her.

"That's right," Felicia added, "the same dresses the rental company let us take to the red carpet for free."

"You said we all looked good at the Christmas ball," Cassidy reminded Bryn.

"And remember your fancy, expensive gown?" Abby narrowed her eyes slightly. "Remember how that made you feel?"

"That's something I'd prefer to forget," Bryn said quietly. "But thanks for reminding me."

"Come on and admit it, Bryn," Abby persisted. "Spending a lot of money did not make you happy. You could've rented your gown and had a much better night."

"I will never wear a rented gown," Bryn declared.

"Fine. What about a gently used gown?"

"Same difference." Bryn glared at her. "I refuse to wear someone else's smelly old dress and you cannot make me."

"Then why not just look at the bargain sites," Abby pleaded. "You might be surprised."

"Are the gowns new?"

"Some of the sites only carry new dresses," Abby assured her. "And some of them have designer labels—at a fraction of the original prices."

Bryn still felt slightly betrayed by her best friend, but with all eyes on her, she felt something else too. Outnumbered. "Fine," she said sharply. "I'll look at the cheap dresses. But I'm not promising anything." Suddenly she was aware that Felicia had been watching her with a sad sort of interest.

That's when Bryn really remembered little Sofia . . . and suddenly felt about two inches tall.

"I'm sorry, Felicia." Bryn let out a long sigh. "That probably sounds all wrong and selfish. And, believe me, it's not because of Sofia. I just like what I like, that's all." She thought for a moment. "But here's what I'll do." She turned to Abby. "I'll figure a way to do matching funds with my clothing expenses, okay? Whatever I spend on my dress, I'll put into your silly challenge, okay?"

"Okay." Abby just nodded. "Whatever works for you and helps Sofia."

"Good." Bryn tried to act like this was no big deal, like she was perfectly okay with the idea of rented or used formal wear, but the truth was she was not. Even though she'd promised to consider a "cheap" gown, she knew she would not settle for shoddy. Sure, Abby was right about the gown fiasco at the Christmas ball, but that was only because Bryn had been teased for looking like she was wearing a bridal gown. Just because it was white. No, not white. It was cream. But for whatever reason, the rumor had gotten started that she was wearing a bridal gown, and that had ruined everything.

Although Bryn no longer felt the excitement she had earlier, she decided not to let this moment pass without getting a little bit of feedback on the dresses she'd selected. "Even if you all insist on wearing secondhand dresses, can you at least look at the ones I've picked out?" She reached for Cass's iPad again. "I found something for everyone. And, really, part of the fun of prom is planning what we'll wear. Even if you insist on rental gowns, we can still talk about it. Can't we?"

To her relief, they all agreed to look at the designs she'd picked out, but getting them to agree on anything was like herding cats. If someone wanted a long gown, the girl next to her wanted a short one. If one wanted something simple and classic, the other one wanted something with layers and details.

"See," Emma proclaimed, "we will be just like the *real* red carpet." She produced her phone and started to show them the photos she'd taken down in Beverly Hills. "There's Lupita in a pastel gown. And Jennifer Lawrence in that strapless tomato-orange number."

"But look, they're all wearing long gowns," Bryn pointed out. "That's why I think we should probably all go with long too."

"But some of us don't look that great in long gowns," Emma argued. "Felicia and I are both petite. We look better in short dresses."

"I say let everyone wear what they want," Cassidy said. "Emma's right about the red carpet, they're wearing all kinds of styles and colors."

"And here's someone in a short dress." Emma pointed to a photo of a woman in a green satin cocktail dress.

"Who is that?" Bryn peered down at the photo.

"I don't know," Emma admitted. "Someone's date maybe."

"Well, all the real stars are wearing full-length gowns," Bryn told them. "That's what I plan on doing."

"Me too," Devon agreed.

Bryn did a quick search on the iPad. "Look at the Olsen twins." She pointed to a group of photos. "They're both really petite and they look great in long gowns." She frowned. "Well, some of the gowns look good. I think you just have to make the right choice." She was just starting an informative lecture about style and why some gowns made everyone look short and fat while other styles did just the opposite, but before she could finish, the bell rang and it was time to go to class.

Okay, that had not gone like she'd hoped it would. She understood that Abby was only trying to help Sofia by introducing her silly budget blog idea. But somehow Bryn had to exert some kind of quality control over the fashion portion of this big dance. It would be so pathetic if everyone showed up at prom looking like they'd shopped at a thrift store bargain rack.

Check this out," Emma told Cassidy when they met up in the art and graphics department after school.

Cassidy studied the promposal poster that Emma had been working on and nodded. "That looks really good, Em. How'd you get a photo of the bike and camping gear taken up in the mountains like that?"

Emma explained how she'd photoshopped the prize photos over an outdoor scene. "Mr. Rajini helped me with it. Not bad, eh?"

"I like the caption too." Cassidy read the words on top. "See how far a promposal can really take you." On the bottom of the poster were details about winning the prize with the most creative promposal.

"Mrs. Dorman is organizing an online vote for the student body." Cassidy picked up a glossy poster. "Are these ready to go up now?"

"That's why you're here." Emma handed her a roll of

masking tape. "Let's plaster them all over the places where the guys like to hang most." She made a face. "Not that it'll do much good. I already gave Isaac a heads-up about this. I thought it might tempt him to come up with a promposal, but I'm not holding my breath."

"Maybe it takes time to get a really good promposal going," Cassidy said as they headed down the hall.

"Well, I'm starting to dream up some pretty good ones myself," Emma confessed as they started to tape a poster next to the guys' restroom. "I just hope I don't have to use them."

"But maybe you'd win the bike."

"Maybe." Emma brightened.

It was 4:30 by the time they finished hanging the last poster. "We better hurry on over to your grandma's," Cassidy told Emma as they got their stuff from their lockers. "Bryn plans to get Devon there by six."

"That was nice of Bryn to take Devon dress shopping with her," Emma said as they headed outside. "I could tell that Devon was feeling blue. And I felt like such a rat when she casually mentioned her birthday this morning and we all acted like it was no big deal."

"Yeah, me too. Poor Devon."

"Well, she's probably having fun looking at prom gowns." Cassidy unlocked her car. "Although shopping with Bryn is not for the faint of heart."

"I'm sure Devon can handle it."

"Did you finish that painting for her?"

"Yeah. I stashed it at my grandma's yesterday, along with some balloons and crepe paper that was left over from a party at Mom's work."

"And your grandma really didn't mind making us dinner?"

"No, she insisted," Emma assured her. "But I promised we'd do the setting up. Bryn and Abby can do cleanup."

"Do you think Devon will be surprised?"

"I think she'll be shocked. No one has said a peep about it."

"Well, hopefully Bryn won't open her mouth either." Cassidy turned into the driveway, then backed out. "I guess I should park a ways away, huh?"

As they went inside, Cassidy held up the package that she'd wrapped yesterday. "I'm not sure what Devon will think of this," she said with uncertainty.

"What is it?" Emma asked.

"A Bible."

Emma looked surprised.

"I know," Cassidy said. "She'll probably hate it. But it's in really easy-to-understand language and it has lots of study helps."

"I think that's a nice gift," Emma assured her. "Even if Devon acts like it's not so great . . . well, don't take her too seriously. Remember, she's Devon."

"Right." Even so, Cassidy was already regretting her impulsive choice. She didn't want Devon to think she was preaching at her. Cassidy said a silent prayer as she followed Emma inside, setting the package on a living room table where several other wrapped presents were already waiting, some from Emma's grandma and one that looked like the painting Emma had made. Even though it was silly, Cassidy took the time to bury her package beneath the other gifts. At least she could delay the disappointment.

"It's so sweet of you girls to do this for Devon," Emma's grandma said as they joined her in the kitchen. "She's been very quiet lately and I've been worried that she might be sad."

"Or maybe she's just thinking about things," Emma said.

"Well, her mother never calls." Emma's grandma sadly shook her head. "I've told Devon to go ahead and make the first move and call her mom, but she just refuses."

"What a beautiful cake," Cassidy said when she spied the layer cake. The frosting was a buttery yellow and it was decorated with real flowers and hot pink birthday candles. "Devon should like that."

"And it's carrot cake," Emma's grandma told her. "Devon's favorite."

"Is that lasagna?" Emma asked as she peeked in the oven window.

Her grandma confirmed this, then sent Cassidy and Emma into the dining room to set the table. "I've put out a nice linen tablecloth and the good china," she called. "And I've got a bouquet of yellow rosebuds and some pink candles for the candelabra too."

"Pretty formal shindig," Emma said as she and Cassidy began to smooth out the tablecloth. "I'm starting to feel jealous. Grandma hasn't gotten out the good china for me."

"You're not seventeen yet," her grandma called from the kitchen.

Emma laughed. "Oh, I didn't know that was the magic number."

After the table was set, Emma and Cassidy blew up balloons and draped the living room with crepe paper. It was a little before six when Abby and Felicia arrived, and that's when they turned off all the lights and hid in the shadows, waiting to surprise Devon.

"Do you think she'll be surprised?" Felicia whispered in the darkness.

"I hope so," Emma said quietly.

"But, knowing Devon, she might play it cool and act like she expected it," Cassidy told her.

"I hear something," Abby warned them.

The door opened and, as they'd previously agreed, everyone silently counted to five and then Emma turned on the light switch and they all leaped out, yelling, "Surprise!"

"What!" Devon leaped back, obviously surprised.

"Happy birthday," they started calling, rushing out to hug their shocked friend. Bryn was coming in behind her now, and suddenly Devon was crying. She wasn't just crying, she was sobbing.

"Oh, Devon," Emma said with worried eyes.

"Did we frighten you?" Felicia asked.

"Are you okay?" Emma's grandma said with concern.

"I—I'm fine," Devon sobbed. "I—I'm just so surprised."

"Well, that's the point," Cassidy said as she hugged her again.

"But we didn't mean to scare you to death," Abby assured her.

"I never had a surprise party before." Devon blew her nose on the tissue that Emma's grandma had handed her. "In fact, I never had a real birthday party before."

"No real birthday party?" Cassidy asked.

"Now that you mention it, I don't ever remember you having a birthday party either," Emma admitted.

"Anyway, sorry to fall apart." Devon stood up straighter. "This is really sweet, you guys. Thanks!"

"It was Cassidy's idea," Emma said.

Devon turned to Cassidy with a slightly astonished expression. "Really? You thought of this?"

Cassidy shrugged. "Well, when I heard it was your birthday . . . it seemed like a good idea."

Devon hugged Cassidy again. "Thanks, Cass, you really are a friend."

Cassidy just nodded.

As the party progressed into dinner, Cassidy could see that Devon was really having a good time, but as the group moved to the living room to open presents, Cassidy was feeling nervous. As Devon opened the first gifts—slightly frivolous items, but obviously things she liked—Devon graciously expressed thanks.

"Oh, Emma," she said as she peeled the paper away from the painting. "I love this. Did you really paint it yourself?"

"I was trying to imitate van Gogh," Emma confessed, "but maybe I should stick to my own style."

Devon held up the painting for everyone to see, and Emma looked relieved as they all praised it. Cassidy was feeling even more nervous because hers was the only gift remaining. But just as she was reaching for it, Bryn held a shiny gold bag toward Devon. "Now this!" Bryn announced with a twinkle in her eyes.

Devon took the bag and, opening it, slid out what appeared to be a shoe box. "Are you kidding?" she said as she removed the lid. She held up a pair of gorgeous strappy silver sandals. "How did you do that?" she asked Bryn.

"When you went to use the restroom, I bought them and they let me slip them into my oversized bag. I thought for sure you'd notice how fat it looked."

"I never even noticed." Devon was already pulling off her shoes and slipping her feet into the silver sandals. "They're perfect."

"And they'll go with almost any prom gown," Bryn proclaimed.

"One gift left," Emma announced just as Cassidy was considering tucking the last package under a couch cushion. "It's from Cass."

Cassidy controlled herself from rolling her eyes. "And if you don't like it, I think you can exchange it," she said quietly.

Devon took her time to unwrap it and when she saw that it was a Bible, her expression grew serious. Or maybe it was grim. Cassidy wasn't sure.

"What is it?" Abby asked.

"A Bible," Emma told her quietly.

"Thanks, Cass," Devon said in a somber tone.

"Really, you can return it," Cassidy assured her. "I just thought that maybe you didn't have one and I really like having—"

"I'm going to keep it," Devon told her. "I like it. I really do."

Cassidy let out a small relieved sigh.

"You guys are the best," Devon told them. "This is the best birthday party ever."

"You said it was your only birthday party," Abby reminded her.

"Yeah, so it could be the worst one ever too," Emma teased.

"No way." Devon shook her head. "It's the best. I swear it is."

"And we still have birthday cake," Emma's grandma announced.

As they went into the dining room for dessert, Cassidy felt relatively certain that Devon had meant what she'd said. After all, Devon was the kind of girl who always spoke her mind. She'd said that she liked the Bible and that she intended to keep it. That was enough for Cass.

As much as Devon liked being the center of attention, she was somewhat relieved when the focus of her birthday party switched over to a discussion of how they were going to get the guys to step up and start delivering some promposals. Oh, for sure, this surprise party had been amazing. And her friends were amazing. But for the first time in her life, Devon felt like she could do with a little less of the limelight. That felt surprisingly good.

"I know we said we were not going to use any Dating Games tricks to get the guys to take us to prom," Bryn was saying. "But with prom getting pushed so far up, we might need to resort to some tactical maneuvers to get this thing off the ground."

Abby laughed. "You make it sound like warfare."

"It is like warfare," Bryn told her. "Right now, it's the guys against us. How long do you think they'll hold out on their silly boycott anyway? I honestly thought they'd be over it by now. But so far no tickets have been sold. No one has committed to going to prom. And every single day is costing us."

"Costing us?" Felicia looked confused.

"Not literally," Bryn admitted. "But it does take away some of the fun. And it contributes to the stress. Wouldn't it be nice if we all knew who was taking us to prom right now?"

"I don't know," Cassidy told her. "Maybe it would be more fun to just let things take their course."

"What if that means you don't go to prom at all?" Bryn asked.

Cassidy shrugged. "That's fine."

"Really?" Bryn looked shocked.

"Maybe I'd get a girls' group together," Cassidy told her. "That could be fun."

"I agree," Felicia said suddenly. "It might be more fun to go with a group of girls. Less pressure, you know?"

"That's a good point," Emma told her.

"But what about a promposal?" Bryn asked. "And the prize?"

"Maybe a girl will win it," Cassidy suggested.

"And since the girls are the ones who've worked the hardest on all this, maybe that would be more fair," Devon said, finally joining the conversation.

Bryn looked stunned. "Seriously, Devon, are you siding with them now? Of all the girls, I figured you would stick with me on this."

Devon felt uncertain now. Bryn was right; this was a little out of character for her. But she just wanted to be honest. "I guess I'm not feeling all that desperate right now, Bryn. Like who cares if a guy asks you to prom or not? What's the big deal? We can still dress up and go on our own. And it might be more fun that way." She grinned at her friends. "Really, you guys are the best. I'd be honored to have all of you for my prom dates."

"That's the spirit," Cassidy told her.

"Yeah," Emma agreed. "Here's to girl power."

Just like that, everyone except Bryn was totally on board with the idea that they might just go to prom as a bunch of girlfriends. And, really, what was wrong with that?

Because it was a school night and because some of them had homework, the amazing party finally had to come to an end. Although some of the girls offered to stay to clean up, Devon insisted that they let her do it.

"But it's your birthday," Cassidy told her.

"Yeah, so I get to call the shots, right?" Devon winked. "And I want to clean up. Okay? And while I'm cleaning up I'll be replaying the way you guys scared the spit out of me when I walked in the door." She laughed, pushing them toward the front door and thanking them all over again.

She used her "call the shots" line on Grandma Betty too, insisting that the older woman call it a night. "I really want to do this," she told her. "Unless you don't trust me with your good china. I promise to be careful."

Thankfully, Grandma Betty didn't argue. But before she went to her room, she gave Devon another big hug and a kiss on the cheek. "You're a *good* girl, Devon Fremont, and I thank the good Lord that you're part of my life," she said in a serious tone. "Happy birthday, darling!"

As Devon loaded the dishwasher, she felt equally thankful for Grandma Betty—and for her friends. And as she carefully washed and dried the delicate china, she felt like something inside her was clicking into place. She wasn't sure what it was exactly, but she could definitely feel it. Maybe it was part of growing up, turning seventeen. Or maybe it had something to do with her heart . . . and God . . . but something in her was changing. And it felt good.

• • ● • •

Devon was aware that some of the girls, Bryn in particular, were under the illusion that Devon might go to prom with Harris. Probably because she'd gone to the Christmas ball with him. And really, as friends they got along pretty well.

"I can ask Harris for you," Bryn had told Devon while they were prom shopping on Devon's birthday. But Devon had persuaded Bryn to keep that idea on hold for now. Although Devon liked Harris well enough, she suspected that his interest in her was fairly minimal. In fact, she'd caught him looking at Amanda Norton a couple of times and she wouldn't be surprised if those two went to prom together.

And it wasn't as if she really cared. As obsessed as Bryn was with lining up dates for prom, Devon had meant what she'd said at her birthday party last night—she would be just fine going with a bunch of girls. In fact, it might be fun. Besides that, Devon really felt like she had some unfinished business to attend to. Something she wanted to take care of before she even considered going to prom. But she knew it wouldn't be easy.

Every morning Devon had gone out of her way to avoid a certain person in her first-period English class. Leonard Mansfield. To be fair, Leonard went out of his way to avoid her as well. And who could blame him? When Devon considered how she'd treated him at the masquerade ball last fall, the fit she'd thrown when she realized he was her "blind date" and how she'd left him high and dry at the dance, well, she felt genuinely ashamed of herself. To be fair, this was only a recent revelation and something she had admitted to no one. Not even Grandma Betty.

This morning, Devon didn't plan to avoid Leonard. And knowing that he was always the first one in his seat, sitting far in the back—probably to avoid crossing paths with her—she made sure to get to class early today. Sure enough, there was Leonard sitting in back with his nose in a book.

"Hey Leonard," she said quietly.

Leonard looked up with big brown eyes, reminding her of the clichéd deer caught in the headlights. "Huh?"

She slipped into the seat next to him, leaning over. "I know you probably hate me," she whispered. "And I can't blame you for that. The way I treated you last fall, at the masquerade ball—well, it was really, really bad. I was totally rude and selfish and stupid and I just wanted to tell you that I'm sorry."

Leonard blinked, then looked all around, almost as if he suspected there was a hidden camera or something.

"I'm not punking you," she assured him. "I just want you to know I'm truly sorry. And maybe someday . . . well, maybe you can forgive me. Okay?"

He still looked stunned, but at least he nodded. "Uh, yeah—okay."

She stuck out her hand. "Friends?"

He looked uneasy, as if he thought she'd jerk her hand back or pull some other rude stunt, but eventually he reached out his hand and she shook it. "Honestly, Leonard, I am sorry." She released his hand and smiled.

He nodded again, and this time he looked a little more at ease. "Thanks, Devon," he muttered. "That means a lot to me."

"Thank you, Leonard. And I mean it—I hope you'll consider me your friend now."

He gave a slightly uncertain nod. "Yeah, sure."

Since other kids were entering the room and taking their seats, Devon considered moving. But then she turned back to Leonard. "Mind if I sit back here?"

He shrugged.

And so she remained there, even though she could tell that kids were looking curiously at her. She suspected that many of them knew how she—dressed as Juliet—had rudely dumped Leonard, her Romeo, at the masquerade ball. They probably even knew that she'd been drunk. Her cheeks flushed to remember how stupid she'd been back then. And even though it was only about half a year since all that happened, she felt like it was ancient history. She never wanted to go back there.

After class ended, she turned back to Leonard and smiled. To her relief, he returned her smile. "See ya around," she said cheerfully as she gathered her stuff.

"Yeah, see you, Devon." His eyes lit up. "And thanks."

"Thank you," she told him as she stood to leave.

As Devon walked to her next class, she couldn't believe how good she felt. Who knew that apologizing to someone came with such a good rush? And, really, Leonard seemed like a genuinely nice guy. Why on earth had she been so nasty to him?

It wasn't until her last class, drama, that Devon got an idea. Okay, maybe it was a crazy idea, but Devon knew she was going to do it. It would take a bit of planning and a bit of luck, but she was determined to pull it off. She confided her idea to the drama teacher, Mr. Ramsay, and after swearing him to secrecy, she talked him into loaning her something. "I promise to return it in perfect condition tomorrow," she assured him.

• ● ● ● •

The next morning, dressed in her full-length black coat, Devon found Isaac McKinley, who was also in her first-period English class. Acting like a foreign spy, she pulled him aside and asked him to do a favor.

"What is it?" he asked curiously.

She quickly explained the details to him. "Just make sure you get a good seat," she said finally. "I need to come in a few minutes late."

He chuckled. "I can't wait to see this—and to record it too." He held up his iPhone. "See ya in there, Juliet."

"Oh, yeah." Devon took a deep breath and, steadying herself, she started to unbutton her coat. The final bell rang and the halls were relatively quiet as she tossed the bulky coat to the floor and did some final adjustments to the Juliet costume that she'd borrowed from Mr. Ramsay. "Here goes nothing," she said under her breath.

Holding her head high, Devon opened the door to the English room. A couple of kids looked up and giggled and then she began. "Oh, Romeo, Romeo, wherefore art thou, dear Romeo?" She strolled across the front of the room, enjoying the spectacle she was making. Then she stopped and, holding her hand over her mouth, she said, "Oops, I mean, Leonard, Leonard, wherefore art thou, dear Leonard?" She turned to Leonard, who was staring at her with a horrified expression.

But she continued going down the row toward him, calling his name. When she reached his desk, she fell to her knees. "Dear Leonard," she said with what she hoped looked like genuine affection, "please, tell me that now that you have forgiven me, you will do me the favor of going to prom with me. Please, dear Leonard, I beg you for mercy. Do not deny me this heartfelt request." With hands clasped she peered up at him.

Leonard's face seemed to grow even paler as he stared at her in horror, but he said nothing and the classroom was so quiet Devon thought she could hear Leonard's heart pounding.

"Please, Leonard," she pressed on, "do not leave me hanging here like this. I am asking you to go to prom with me. Please, say yes, Leonard."

He locked eyes with her as if considering this.

"Come on, Leonard," someone called out. "Tell Jules you'll take her to prom."

"Yeah, Leonard. Say yes."

Leonard's head bobbed up and down and he finally said, "Okay, I guess I can take you, Devon—uh, I mean, Juliet."

Everyone clapped as she leaped to her feet and hugged him. "Thank you, Leonard," she cried. "You will not be sorry."

She hurried up to the front of the classroom, assuring the teacher that she would be back in five minutes. "Sorry about that," she murmured.

He laughed. "It's okay. I kind of enjoyed the show."

As Devon grabbed up her coat and dashed back to the

bathroom where she'd stashed her school clothes, she felt giddy. Had she really just done that? Asked nerdy Leonard Mansfield to prom? What would her friends say when they heard?

She laughed. Really, did she care?

It was the Monday of the week before spring break, less than two weeks to prom, and Emma was feeling uneasy. Oh, she wanted to act nonchalant. She admired how Cassidy acted like she could take it or leave it when it came to receiving a promposal. Just this morning, Cassidy had been seriously talking about going to prom with a group of girls. And Emma had tried to appear interested. She wished she was interested. But what Emma really wanted was for Isaac to surprise her with a fabulous promposal. Really, was that too much to ask?

She couldn't believe it when Isaac had shown her the hilarious video he'd taken of Devon playing Juliet and asking Leonard to prom. And it wasn't just Devon's unexpected promposal that stunned Emma. It was the fact that Isaac had the gall to show her someone else's promposal without even considering how that made her feel. *What about* your *promposal?* she wanted to demand. Fortunately she just managed to laugh, complimenting him on his good camera work. "Devon might've just won herself a bike," she'd told Isaac. And at the rate the other promposals were *not* coming in, Devon really might win.

Bryn complained about it at lunch that day. "What if Devon and Leonard are the only couple at prom?"

"Then we'll be crowned King and Queen," Devon teased. "And I will win the bike."

"And the prom will make no money," Abby pointed out. "And FYI, Devon, Northwood doesn't have prom king. Just prom queen."

"Let's put a lid on it," Emma said quietly. "Here comes Felicia." She waved to Felicia as she quickly relayed the latest. "She's feeling pretty bad about Sofia right now. The chemo kicked in and Sofia's hair started falling out, so they shaved her head this weekend. Felicia showed me a photo and Sofia was smiling brightly, but it was still sad."

The girls all greeted Felicia and, to Emma's relief, kept the prom talk upbeat and positive. When Bryn inquired about Sofia, Felicia produced her phone and showed them the photo. "She's really got a good attitude," Felicia told them. "I even offered to shave my head in solidarity, but she wouldn't let me. She said I needed my hair to go to prom." Felicia frowned as she slipped her phone back into her bag. "Not that I'm holding my breath."

Emma noticed Isaac and Marcus coming their way. Occasionally some guys would join them at their table, but not so much since the prom wars had begun. Emma repressed the urge to sneer at Isaac. For all she knew he could be here for a reason—and he was pulling something from his pocket. Was he about to ask her to prom?

To her dismay it was only his phone, which he was aiming at Marcus. She turned to look at Marcus, wondering if he was about to do a promposal. But he simply stood in front of their table with a goofy grin. He looked handsome in a cowboy sort of way with his plaid western shirt, jeans, and harness boots.

"Felicia," he said in a rather loud voice. "Come here!"

Felicia looked embarrassed, but stood. "What?"

"Go ahead." Bryn gave Felicia a gentle shove toward Marcus.

"What's going—"

Just then Marcus reached up to his collar. He ripped his shirt open, the snaps releasing to show his bare chest. Inked carefully and rather artistically there were three words:

Felicia

Marcus

Prom?

Felicia squealed as she jumped up and down. "Yes, yes!" she cried. Then she hugged Marcus, and Emma could see tears in her eyes.

"Way to go, dude!" Devon was on her feet, slapping Marcus on the back as he snapped up his shirt. "It's nice to see that at least one of the guys isn't a coward."

Felicia looked at Isaac. "Did you get it? Did you record it?"

He nodded as he studied his phone. "Yep. It's all here." He looked at Marcus. "I just sent it to your phone." He nodded to Felicia. "And yours too."

"You can enter the contest," Felicia told Marcus.

"Yeah, but it probably won't beat Devon's." Marcus tipped his head to Devon. "Nicely done, Devon."

"Thanks." She grinned. "I figured someone needed to get the ball rolling. And hey, if I win that bike, you won't hear me complaining."

Emma tried not to look directly at Isaac as the group continued talking and joking about promposals, but all she could think of was that it was hopeless to keep pining away for Isaac. This guy had absolutely no interest in going to prom with her. She'd already hinted to him several times. She'd even complained to him at youth group. And even though he'd acted understanding, like he was going to do something, he had done nothing. Well, she decided, if Isaac didn't want to go to prom with her, maybe it was time to start looking around for someone else. Because suddenly, and inexplicably, Emma really wanted to go to prom. And, as Grandma would say, Isaac was not the only fish in the sea.

After the guys went on their way, the girls congratulated Felicia on her invitation to prom and rewatched the video that Isaac had sent to her phone. Emma was happy for her friend. If anyone needed a promposal today, it was Felicia. What great timing.

"I went ahead and got my dress yesterday," Bryn told them.

"Even though no one's asked you yet?" Abby shook her head.

"I had to get it in order to have time for alterations." Bryn looked at Abby. "You'll be pleased to know that it was on sale and I'll donate the savings to your PBC fund."

"But how can you be so certain you're going to prom?" Emma demanded. "Or are you like Cass—planning to go in a girls' group?"

Bryn wrinkled her nose. "I do not plan to go in a girls' group."

"Bryn could get Jason to ask her," Devon told them. "All she has to do is give him the time of day."

Bryn seemed to consider this. "He wouldn't be my first choice, but hey, he might do in a pinch."

"You'd go with someone you don't even like?" Emma asked.

Bryn seemed to consider this. "Well, to be honest, I'd rather not."

"What about Harris?" Emma suggested—and then suddenly wished that she hadn't, since she was pretty good friends with Harris. Maybe he'd be a good option if Isaac remained stubborn.

Bryn's eyes lit up. "Yeah . . . I've actually been thinking about that. I wouldn't mind going with Harris."

"Want me to drop some hints his way?" Devon offered. "I have him in my economics class."

Bryn nodded firmly. "Yes," she agreed. "That'd be great, Devon. Thanks."

"Or you could just invite him," Cassidy suggested.

Suddenly the girls were all talking about promposals that they thought would be fun. "What about writing it in lipstick on his windshield?" Devon tossed out.

"Or put it out on the school marquee," Abby said. "Unless that's not allowed."

"You could paint it on his locker," Emma suggested. She'd actually considered doing that to Isaac but couldn't work up the nerve. What if he said no?

"Hey, look!" Cassidy pointed over to a table where a bunch of guys were congregated. They all turned to see Mazie Tucker carrying a platter of what looked like cupcakes toward the guys.

"Let's go watch this." Devon was already up. And the rest of the DG followed, clustering around Mazie and her friend who was getting the unfolding event on camera. Emma peered over Cassidy's shoulder to see what the red letters on the white cupcakes spelled out.

Harris?

Prom?

With me?

Mazie's cheeks flushed pink as she waited quietly for Harris to respond to her sweet invitation. Emma knew that Mazie was very shy and to do this in front of everyone—risking public rejection—was really, really brave. And Emma was silently cheering for her.

"Say yes!" Devon urged him.

"Yeah, man," a guy said. "Those cupcakes look yummy."

Harris grinned at Mazie. "Sure, I'd like to go to prom with you."

With a relieved smile, Mazie handed over the cupcakes. "They're red velvet."

"Seriously?" Harris looked surprised. "I *love* red velvet."

Her eyes twinkled. "Yeah, that's what I heard." And now she grabbed the arm of her camera friend and hurried away as the guys dove for the cupcakes.

"Well, I don't think that's going to beat my promposal," Devon said as they walked back to their table. "But I gotta admit it was pretty cool."

"At least people are starting to get on board," Abby said.

"With no time to waste," Bryn said in a dejected tone.

"I guess I don't need to drop hints with Harris now," Devon said.

Bryn just frowned.

"Hey, you should do what I did." Devon poked Bryn's shoulder. "Ask a nice, nerdy guy." She laughed. "Maybe I should create a new holiday: *Ask a nerd to prom day*."

Emma considered this as she walked to class. Maybe she needed to lower her expectations about prom. Just because she liked Isaac didn't mean that she had to go to prom with him. If Devon was okay going with someone like Leonard—who was actually a really nice guy—maybe Emma needed to expand her own search. Not that she was searching exactly.

By the end of the day, Emma had made a decision. She would quit thinking about a prom date. Like Cassidy, she would simply be content with the idea of going to prom with a group of girls. And, really, wouldn't that be fun? Since she'd promised to help her grandma with a garage sale during spring break, she might even make enough money to purchase her own prom ticket. What was wrong with being independent—and hanging with girlfriends—at an event like prom? Cassidy was right—they didn't have to be on the arm of a guy to have a good time. Perhaps they'd have an even better time by not being with a guy.

From now on, Emma was determined to focus all her prom energy on the decorations. And since she was chairing the decorations committee, she would have more than enough to keep her busy for the next couple of weeks.

Emma headed back to the art department, where she'd asked the committee to meet with her after school to help with decorations. Today was their first official meeting and she knew they had no time to waste. Last weekend she'd started a list of easy and inexpensive ideas that she felt would lend themselves to the red carpet theme. She'd even made some sketches.

"Thanks for coming," she told everyone as she stood in front of the small group of students. "As you know, our theme is red carpet and our budget is limited." She held up a large sketch. "The entrance to prom will be set up like this." She explained how a rental company had offered them a discount on the red runner and brass poles to cordon it along the sides. "We'll make glittery gold stars to lay on the red carpet, and we'll use lots of white lights and metallic-toned balloons to make it feel glitzy." She held up another sketch. "We'll create an eight-foot-tall star with more silver and gold balloons and light strings. It will provide the background for photos."

As she continued sharing her ideas with the committee, she was surprised at how enjoyable it felt to be up front and calling the shots—especially in the art arena, a place she felt comfortable. And everyone seemed supportive and agreeable as she assigned various tasks.

"As you guys can see, I'm trying to keep it simple. The main thing is to make it look like a fun and exciting gala without spending too much money, because everything we save goes to help Sofia Ruez." She paused to catch her breath. "But I don't want it to feel cheesy or cheap." Then she told them a little bit about how it felt to be at the real red carpet. By the time they finished the meeting, she knew she had a good team behind her. They could do this!

Still feeling like it had been a successful meeting, Emma took her time to bundle up her sketches and even wrote down a few more notes from some of the ideas that the committee had tossed out. She packed everything into her oversized bag and was just turning off the lights to the art room when she heard the sound of footsteps coming through the breezeway.

To her surprise, it was Isaac—and he still had on his lacrosse uniform. She knew they'd had a match after school. Apparently it was over now. But she couldn't read the expression on his face as he approached her.

"Hey, Isaac." She closed the door behind her.

"Hey." He had what looked like a cup of coffee in his hand as he planted himself in front of her. But there was a strange look in his eyes.

"Is something wrong?" she asked.

"No."

"How was your lacrosse match?"

"We won."

"Good." She gave him a stiff smile. "I just finished a decorations meeting . . . for prom." She wished she'd left off that last phrase.

"Yeah, I know."

"Oh." She just nodded, attempting to step past him.

"Wait." He held the cup of coffee out toward her.

"Huh?"

"This is for you."

"For me?" She felt puzzled as she took the cup from him. "Why?"

"Don't you still like mocha with whipped cream?"

"Yeah, sure. But why are—"

He reached over and gently turned the cup around in her hand. On the side of the white paper cup was the word *PROM?*

She blinked then looked again. "Are you sure this cup is for me?"

He nodded. "Yeah."

"I mean, are you sure this cup is from you? To me?"

He gave her a sheepish smile. "Yeah, Emma. I'm asking you to prom, and I won't blame you for pouring that over my head."

She looked down at the cup. "And waste a perfectly good mocha?"

He chuckled. "So, will you go?"

She waited for a few seconds, acting like she was unsure, then broke into a big grin. "Sure, Isaac, I'd love to. Thanks."

He gave her a relieved smile. "Cool."

"So how did you know I was down here in the art room?" she asked as they walked together.

"Cassidy told me. She was coming to get you to give you a ride. But I told her to go on home and that I'd give you a lift. If that's okay."

"Hey, it's better than riding the activities bus."

"I wanted to explain why it took me so long to ask you," he said quietly as they walked through the locker bay.

This she wanted to hear—so she said nothing.

"At first I was kind of into the prom boycott thing. But then I realized it was pretty childish. And I knew you wanted me to ask you. But I wanted to do it in my own timing . . . my own way. And even though everyone is starting to get into the whole promposal thing—by the way, a bunch of guys were springing them on girls after school—I didn't want to ask you *because* of the contest, you know? I wanted to ask you just because I wanted to ask you, Emma. Does that make sense?"

"It does to me."

"Because I do want to take you to prom—but not to win a contest. I just wanted to ask you in my own way, you know?"

She held up her cup. "This mocha works for me."

"Cool."

As they walked out to Isaac's car, Emma thought Isaac's invitation couldn't have been better. "I'm glad you didn't have anyone record it," she said as they got into his car. "I like that it was just between you and me."

"Yeah," he agreed. "Me too. Besides, we already won the Christmas ball prize. It would be embarrassing to win the prom one too."

She laughed. "Well, no offense, but as much as I'm enjoying this mocha I don't think it could've beaten Devon's Juliet or Marcus's temporary tattoo. Even Mazie's cupcakes would probably get more votes."

"Yeah, I know. And believe it or not, I did spend some time trying to think of something more clever, not to win a prize, but just for fun, you know? But when I saw your face at lunch—when Marcus surprised Felicia—well, I knew I needed to get on this thing fast."

"Well, thanks, Isaac." She sighed as she took another sip of mocha. At least she hadn't told Cassidy that she'd do the girls' group date yet. She was glad to know that she'd truly been willing to do that. She glanced at Isaac. But this was better. Much better.

By Wednesday, Abby was starting to plan a promposal of her own. If Kent wasn't going to ask her, she would simply swallow her pride and ask him. After all, there was no denying that they were friends—and on good enough terms to attend prom together. And she'd already hinted to her parents that she was going and, although Dad acted like Dad, he did give his okay. The only problem now was Kent. If the boy kept dragging his heels, she had no problem jumping in and possibly making a total fool of herself. Best case scenario, she might win a bike. If only she could think of something really fabulous to do. Especially since Kent appeared sadly unmotivated.

But to be fair, she knew the whole track team had been distracted with really hard practices this week. Their first big meet was coming up on Thursday and the whole team was focused on improving times and being in tip-top form. So if Abby did a promposal—and she just might—it would have to wait until Friday. But she was determined that Friday would be her deadline. If she didn't get a yes from Kent, she would resign herself to going to prom with Cassidy . . . and maybe Bryn too since no one had asked her yet.

It hadn't made Abby feel any better to see promposals going off like fireworks all around the school. There had been several first thing this morning, and Olivia Pratt's locker had been flamboyantly decorated with balloons and streamers. There'd been at least five at lunch—including a giant cookie, a singing telegram, and a senior who wasn't a bad juggler. Even after school, there had been squeals and shrieks when Amanda Norton came rushing into the courtyard, urging everyone to go out and look at her car.

Assuming Amanda's car had been in a wreck, Abby and Bryn had run out to see. But, as it turned out, Jason had painted a promposal (hopefully with water-based paint) all over Amanda's pretty little car. Abby had laughed and Bryn had pasted a stiff-looking smile on her face. But as they walked back into the school, Abby could tell that Bryn was not pleased. Abby knew that Bryn had been secretly holding out for Jason to spring a promposal on her. And Abby felt pretty certain that Bryn would've accepted it. Oh, she might've acted like it was beneath her, but she would've said yes.

It seemed that Bryn and Cass and Abby were all in the same boat—dateless for prom. As Abby waited for her turn in the long jump, she fantasized a fabulous scene where her DG girlfriends performed a choreographed dance in the cafeteria. They would be joined by other kids until it turned into an amazing flash dance. Naturally, it would be filmed from a good vantage point. Then Abby's DG friends, wearing denim jackets over white T-shirts, would line up in front of Kent and just as the song ended, they would whip open their jackets to reveal that their T-shirts each had a different letter on the front, spelling out P-R-O-M-?, and finally Abby would open her jacket and her T-shirt would say WITH ME.

Okay, maybe that sort of promposal was too over-the-top, not to mention difficult to pull off—who had time to practice a flash dance? But it was fun to daydream about. Abby realized she was on deck for long jump now. Time to focus on sprinting and positioning her steps—and stretching her arms and flying. Promposals would have to come later. If at all.

Abby ended her track practice back at the high jump pit. A lot of the other kids had already quit for the day, but Abby really wanted to get in a few last jumps while her legs were still warmed up. She'd done some jumps earlier but hadn't been happy with her height. She'd managed to raise her personal best jump two inches in the last couple of weeks, but for some reason she hadn't been able to clear it this afternoon. And the more she pushed herself at the end of practice, the worse it seemed to get. Finally, tired and discouraged, Abby collapsed onto the high jump pit pad and, lying flat on her back, simply looked up at the sky. A few fluffy white clouds were peacefully floating across the clear blue. So peaceful . . . so quiet.

Abby knew that she'd been overly focused on prom lately. And it was kind of weird since that really wasn't who she was. She could blame her obsession on Bryn's influence, but that wouldn't be fair. Abby was old enough to make her own choices. And, to be honest, Abby had enjoyed setting up the PBC blog. She liked being able to encourage students to economize by renting or borrowing formal wear. Already the savings were starting to accumulate. It would be exciting to see how much they could donate to the Sofia fund.

Abby watched a horse-shaped cloud running overhead. Throwing its head and mane back, it raced with cloud-like freedom and abandon. The image of the fluffy white horse was invigorating and exhilarating. And suddenly Abby wanted to imitate it—to run free and wild. She got off the high jump pit and started out, jogging slowly at first, letting the muscles in her legs stretch a bit, and then she was running fast—all the way back to the locker room where she showered and dressed. She'd already texted Bryn to go home without her. Bryn's prom meeting would've ended nearly an hour ago. And then she'd texted her dad to pick her up on his way home from the college where he worked. But that meant that Abby had to wait until nearly six to go home.

As Abby emerged from the girls' locker room, she could hear quiet voices followed by some strains of laughter up toward the gym. Hopefully it wasn't another promposal. She wasn't sure if she could stomach that. But, she decided, if it was, she would be a good sport and be happy for whoever was involved. As she rounded the corner next to the gym, she heard the sound of music playing and suddenly a figure was rushing toward her, but it was too shadowy to see the face.

She wasn't sure whether to run or brace herself for impact, but her feet refused to move. In the same instant, the runner hit the floor, just like he was sliding into first base. He glided over the slick floor's surface, coming to a stop right in front of her. By now she knew it was Kent. He had a huge smile on his face and a gigantic pizza box in his hands.

"Special delivery for Miss Abby Morrison," Kent said with a twinkle in his blue eyes. Someone turned the music off.

"What?" Abby stared down at him in wonder.

"Special delivery," he said again, extending the box toward her. "For Miss Abby Morrison."

"Uh—thank you," she said cautiously.

He was awkwardly climbing to his feet, still holding the flat cardboard box in one hand. "Go ahead and open it," he urged her.

She slowly opened the lid, almost as if she expected something to jump out at her. But there was a perfectly normal-looking pizza. Except that it was enormous and had a heart created from well-placed pepperoni slices. But it was the words written in red felt pen on the inside of the cardboard lid that got her full attention.

Dear Abby,
I know this is cheesy,
But please say you will
Be my date for prom.

Kent

Kent's eyebrows arched hopefully as he waved the aromatic pizza temptingly beneath her nose. How could she possibly resist this?

"Of course I will!" She hungrily snatched a big piece of pizza and grinned. "Thanks, by the way—I'm starving."

They went outside, and while sitting on a bench in front of the athletic center, Abby and Kent and his camera and music crew proceeded to put a pretty good dent in the pizza.

"I really wanted to do something more exciting," Kent confessed as they ate. "But I overheard Barrett Foster saying he was going to ask you to prom at track practice. And I decided I needed to beat him to the punch."

"Really?" Abby tipped her head to one side. "Barrett was going to ask me?"

Kent looked worried. "Would you have gone with him?"

She pursed her lips like she was uncertain. "Well, was his promposal coming with pizza too?"

"Would that have made a difference?" Kent frowned.

Abby chuckled. "No. I would've turned him down."

"So you're glad I asked you?" Kent sounded unsure.

"I am glad," she admitted. "But I had reached the place where I decided it didn't really matter if you asked me or not. I would be content to go to prom with the girls' group that Cassidy keeps saying she's putting together."

Kent looked slightly hurt now. "You'd rather go with the girls than me?"

She laughed. "No, silly. More than anything I wanted to go with you. I just wanted you to *want* to go with me."

He looked relieved. "I do."

Abby stood when she saw her dad's car pulling up. "Mind if I take my dad a piece?" she asked.

Kent closed the lid on the box and handed what was left to her. "I got it for you, Abs. You can do what you like with it."

"Thanks, Kent." She resisted the urge to bend down and give him a kiss. Only on the cheek! But she knew that even a gesture that small might be a bit much for her overly protective dad. Instead, she said good-bye, then hurried to the car.

"Hanging with your guy friends?" Dad said as she slid into the passenger seat beside him.

"Yeah." She held up the pizza box. "Want a piece?"

"Smells good, but I better wait until we get home. Not safe to eat and drive."

"Suit yourself." Abby took another piece. As she ate, she told Dad about Kent's unexpected promposal, complete with pizza. "I don't know if Kent knew that I was ravenous, but it was a pretty good idea."

"So what if his promposal hadn't involved food?" Dad asked. "Would you have still said yes?"

"Oh, Dad." She shook her head. Really, sometimes parents could be so thick. While she was eating pizza with one hand, she used her other hand to text Bryn the good news. By the time they got home, Bryn was calling and demanding to hear all the details of the promposal.

"I'm not really hungry for dinner," she told her dad from the stairway while Bryn waited for her on the phone. "Besides, I have a ton of homework. Maybe you and Mom can just have a quiet dinner for two."

Dad seemed to consider this. "Okay, I'll tell your mom."

As Abby carried her pizza box upstairs, she told Bryn all about Kent's promposal. Naturally, she dragged it out some, probably making it seem better than it really was. But, hey, she'd been hungry. And Kent had delivered.

"I'm so depressed," Bryn finally said.

"Why?" Abby took another bite of pizza, then realized she'd hit her limit, set it down, and closed the box.

"There are only two days until spring break—and I still don't have a date for prom."

"Oh, yeah." Abby sat down on her bed, realizing it was time for some compassion. "With Jason and Harris out of the running . . . where does that leave you?"

"I don't know."

"You could always go with Cassidy's girls' group."

Bryn let out a loud groan.

"Or ask someone yourself." Abby confessed to how she'd been about to do the same thing. "I was giving myself until Friday—to get the track meet behind us—and then I was going to ask Kent."

"Really?"

"Yep. And why not? Lots of girls are doing the asking. And, hey, if I'd done the promposal I was dreaming about, I might've won a bike."

"Really?" Bryn sounded very interested now. "What kind of promposal did you have in mind?"

"Oh, nothing much," Abby said quietly. She was sure Bryn would have no interest in hearing her silly ideas. What Bryn wanted was a date and some encouragement. So Abby spent the next ten minutes trying to cheer up her best friend. She even told her about the running-free cloud horse, hoping it would seem like something of an epiphany. But Bryn didn't seem to really get it. In the end, she sounded just as discouraged as at the beginning of the call.

"I'm sure you'll think of something," Abby finally said. "I hate to go, but I've got a bunch of homework that's calling my name."

"Yeah . . . me too . . . thanks for listening."

As Abby hung up her phone, she felt sorry for Bryn. Sorry and frustrated. And it wasn't the first time. Why did Bryn always have such unrealistic expectations about almost everything? She'd get these crazy, grandiose dreams—that always needed perfect wardrobe and accessories—and it seemed like most of the time, Bryn was let down in the end. Abby thought by now Bryn would learn. It wasn't like she wanted

Bryn to give up all her dreams, but she did wish Bryn could find some kind of solid middle ground. Then again, maybe that wouldn't be Bryn—and Abby had to admit that Bryn often brought a little more sparkle and fun into their lives.

As Abby opened her math book, she wondered if there might be a way that the DG could help Bryn out. It was ironic that Bryn would even need the DG's help in getting a date for prom. But maybe she did.

By Friday, Cassidy had a group of eight girls interested in going to prom together. Everyone would buy their own tickets, and since Kelsey Chase wanted to arrive in style, they'd all agreed to split the limo rental between them. There'd been a little bickering over dresses—Miranda Sanders wanted all the girls to wear cocktail-length dresses while some of the girls had their hearts set on long gowns—but for the most part the girls seemed happy about going "stag" to prom.

"You're welcome to join us," Cassidy told Bryn as they exited their English class together. "If you did, I'd nominate you as fashion consultant." She laughed as she explained about the dress-length controversy. "I keep telling them that it doesn't matter and that everyone should just wear what they want. But Miranda already has a short dress and she's afraid she'll be the only one."

Bryn's brow was creased and Cassidy didn't think it was

over the dress-length question. "Who are the girls going to dance with at prom?" Bryn asked in a flat tone.

"They don't have to dance with anyone," Cassidy pointed out. "I mean, unless it's a slow dance, who really pays attention to that anyway?"

"Yeah . . . I guess that's true."

"So anyway, you should consider joining us, Bryn. I think it's going to be fun."

Bryn stopped walking at the edge of the courtyard and turned to peer intently at Cassidy. "So you've totally given up on going with a guy to prom?"

Cassidy shrugged. "I guess so."

"I thought you wanted to go with Lane."

She shrugged again. "I'd considered doing a promposal myself, but then I got to thinking that if Lane wanted to go to prom—I mean, *with me*—he probably would've asked me by now."

Bryn's brows arched. "So you think Lane *doesn't* want to go with you?"

"That seems like the obvious conclusion."

"So . . . what if *someone else* asked Lane to prom? Would you be jealous?"

Cassidy frowned. Okay, the truth was she'd probably be a little bit jealous, but she wasn't prepared to admit it. "Why are you asking me that?" She peered curiously at Bryn, but before Bryn said a word, Cassidy knew the answer. "You're going to ask Lane to prom?" Cassidy demanded. "*Seriously?*"

"Well, if you're not . . . why can't I?" Bryn made an apologetic smile.

"What about the DG rules?" Cassidy asked. "Remember the one about no boyfriend stealing?"

"Are you saying that Lane's your boyfriend?"

Cassidy pursed her lips then slowly shook her head.

"So is he fair game then?" Bryn asked.

Suddenly Cassidy wondered if she should throw together some kind of a last-minute promposal for Lane. Sure, it wouldn't be good enough to win her that bike, but if it secured Lane as her date for prom, maybe it would be okay. And it would keep Bryn from going with Lane. Because, honestly, Cassidy knew that the girls' group date wouldn't be nearly as much fun if she had to watch Bryn and Lane together. "I—uh—I don't know," Cassidy told Bryn.

"Because I don't want to step on your toes," Bryn said with a sincere expression. "Really, Cass, if you think you're going to ask Lane to prom, just tell me and I'll back off."

Before Cassidy could respond, the sound of a loud trumpet blast made them both jump.

"Look at that!" Bryn cried as she pointed to the other end of the courtyard. Cassidy turned in time to see George Henley dressed like a knight and riding a stick horse. Lifting his knees high, he pretended that the galloping horse was hard to control. And, of course, he was being followed by a camera-wielding friend.

"Looking for Lady Madeline!" George yelled out. "Anyone seen Lady Madeline?"

"She's right here," a girl's voice answered. She was tugging a slightly embarrassed Madeline out into the center of the courtyard.

George galloped up to Madeline and, dismounting his horse, made a deep bow. "Lady Madeline, I am your servant."

Madeline giggled nervously.

George stood up and produced a long, pointed strip of

green paper. "I have slain the dragon for you, my lady." He handed her the strip. "Here is his tail."

Madeline took the paper dragon tail and appeared to be reading something written on it. She looked up and grinned at George. "Yes!" she told him.

"*Hurrah!*" George gave a fist pump to the cameraman. "Lady Madeline has graciously agreed to attend prom with me!" And now he made a deep bow for the camera, and everyone watching in the courtyard clapped and cheered.

But the warning bell rang and it was time to hurry to class. As Cassidy took her seat, she wondered about her conversation with Bryn. They'd never really wrapped it up. And for all Cassidy knew, Bryn could be planning her promposal right now. Cassidy knew Bryn well enough to know that when that girl set her mind to something, it was hard to stop her. How would Cassidy feel if Bryn succeeded at getting Lane to take her to prom? Oh, she'd try to act like it didn't matter—and Bryn was right, Lane was not Cassidy's boyfriend—but even so it seemed wrong-wrong-wrong for Bryn to go after him.

And if that was how Bryn planned to play this thing, maybe it was time for Cassidy to step in first. Instead of doing her math, Cassidy decided to make a short list of easy ideas for a promposal. She knew that Lane loved peanut M&Ms—what if she got several packages from the vending machine then wrote out the word PROM with them on a paper plate? But how would she present it to him? And what if the colorful round balls slid out of place and she ended up looking totally ridiculous? And, really, why was she wasting time on this when she should be doing her math?

By lunchtime, Cassidy had gone back and forth like a Ping-Pong ball—yes, she was definitely going to ask Lane to prom and then no, she was absolutely not going to ask him. Talk about indecisive. Why couldn't she make up her mind?

Her only consolation, as she joined her friends at their usual lunch table, was that it didn't appear that Bryn had invited Lane to prom . . . yet. At least she wasn't talking about it. And Cassidy knew that Bryn would not be able to keep the news to herself if she and Lane were actually going to prom together. Even so, Cassidy still didn't know if she could bring herself to ask Lane, although she'd figured out a way to adhere the M&Ms. She could get a peanut butter and crackers packet from the vending machine and use the peanut butter to glue the M&Ms in place. And maybe she would . . . as soon as she finished lunch.

"Did you guys see George's promposal this morning?" Bryn asked the girls. She pointed at Devon with a sly expression. "I think that boy might've just beat you out of a pretty red bicycle." She described the promposal, making it sound even grander than it had actually been.

Devon frowned. "That totally stinks. I noticed Mrs. Dorman uploaded our promposals onto the website yesterday. I'll bet George got the idea for the costume when he saw mine."

"Well, I think yours was better," Cassidy assured her. "I'd vote for Juliet over the dragon slayer in a heartbeat."

"Thank you." Devon smirked at Bryn.

Cassidy was just opening her lunch bag when she heard the sound of a guitar playing behind her—and not coming through the cafeteria's speakers either. This music was live.

"Hey!" Emma pointed over Cassidy's shoulder. "Check it out."

Both Cassidy and Bryn turned around to see Lane just a

few feet behind them, quietly strumming a guitar. Cassidy knew that Lane had been taking guitar lessons this year, but she'd never actually heard him play. He kept his head down, focusing on his fingers and the strings and not even sounding too bad. But Cassidy could tell by his slightly rosy cheeks, this boy was totally out of his comfort zone. And judging by Isaac, who was recording the impromptu performance on his phone, Lane was up to something.

"What's he doing?" Abby whispered.

"Is this a promposal?" Felicia asked quietly.

"Sure looks like it." Bryn giggled in a way that seemed to suggest she thought Lane was here for her. And maybe he was. Knowing Bryn, it was entirely possible that she'd asked someone to put Lane up to this. If Lane had thought he had a chance to take someone as pretty as Bryn to prom, he might be willing to humiliate himself a little.

Cassidy took her eyes off Lane to study Bryn. She was clearly amused and enjoying this. Did she think that Lane was playing for her? Was he? Cassidy turned back to Lane now. If he was about to sing to Bryn, she needed to brace herself. She needed to act like this was perfectly fine. After all, she had the girls' group—that would be fun. Why should she care if Bryn and Lane wanted to go to prom together?

Lane looked up from the guitar, and to Cassidy's surprise, he seemed to be staring directly at her as he came closer to their table. By now a small crowd of onlookers had gathered, but Lane just kept on playing, almost like he didn't care. Then he smiled at Cassidy and started to sing a funny little song.

> Oh Cassidy, oh Cassidy,
> You're my friend, can't you see?

I might be slow but hope you know
Just how much you mean to me.

Oh Cassidy, oh Cassidy,
You really are the girl for me.
I need to know, please don't say no,
Tell me you will go with me.

Then Lane flipped his guitar over to show that he'd taped the word PROM? on the back of his guitar. He looked hopefully at her and she leaped to her feet and hugged him. "Yes!" she declared. "I'd be glad to."

Everyone clapped and cheered. Lane grinned happily and, thanks to popular demand, he played her song again. After he was finished with his promposal, Cassidy walked with him to the music department, to return the guitar he'd borrowed for her song.

"So I heard that you thought I was never going to ask you," Lane said as he put the guitar back into the case.

"Where'd you hear that?"

"Bryn told me." He snapped it closed, then slid it onto a shelf.

"She did?" Cassidy was confused. Here she'd been imagining Bryn was out to steal Lane away from her—and now this? "What did Bryn say to you?"

"Just that you were planning to go to prom with a bunch of goofy girls and if I wanted to take you, I'd better step up." He gave her a sheepish smile. "I'd been working on that song and wanted to get it down better before I actually sang it."

"I thought you sang it brilliantly," she told him.

"Thanks. I've been working on it for the past week, but

I didn't really think I could pull it off." He laughed. "But I am glad it's over with."

So Bryn had been the boot on his behind, getting him to perform his promposal even though he hadn't felt ready. Who knew?

• ● ⬤ ● •

Cassidy happily told her parents about Lane's promposal that night. She even showed them the video that Isaac had sent to her after school. As a result, Mom was over the moon to do some prom gown shopping. And even though Cassidy wasn't much of a shopper, she agreed.

On Saturday morning, Cassidy explained about Abby's Prom Budget Challenge, and Dad was so impressed with the idea that he increased Cassidy's prom budget.

"So if you shop frugally, like you planned, you should be left with a tidy little sum to contribute to the little Ruez girl," Dad said as he doled out some more cash. "I really like the way you and your friends are handling your prom. Very generous . . . and mature."

On the way to town, Cassidy was wishing that they could wrap up the gown shopping as quickly as possible. "I'm fine with renting a gown again," she told her mom. "The one I had for the Christmas ball was pretty cool. And I can use those same shoes too."

"Are you saying you want to go straight to Formal Rental Wear?" Mom's voice sounded disappointed.

"Well, not exactly." Cassidy looked down at the list she'd gotten from Abby's website. "There's Angelica's Closet—they sell both new and used gowns."

"I heard that Macy's is having a one-day sale," Mom said. "Plus I have a coupon for an additional 20 percent off."

"But Macy's? Wouldn't that still be a lot more expensive?" Cassidy replied.

"Oh, I don't know." Mom chuckled. "Besides, what if I chipped in a little extra money?"

Cassidy wasn't sure about this. She had actually liked the idea of being frugally dressed.

"And there's always Dress 4 Less," Mom reminded her. "I noticed they had a pretty big formal wear rack in the back. Want to start there?"

Cassidy could tell that Mom wanted to make this a big shopping day. And as much as Cassidy wanted to go straight for the rental place, she agreed to start at Dress 4 Less. But it didn't take long before they realized the gowns there were pretty picked over and there wasn't much to choose from in Cassidy's size.

So next they went to Angelica's Closet. It was a cute shop and had a pretty good selection of gently used gowns, as well as some really great accessories. But after a fairly long hunt and even trying on a few things, nothing really seemed quite right. And the prices weren't as low as Cassidy had hoped they'd be. Most of the dresses she liked were around a hundred dollars, and the designer ones were even more.

"Formal Rental Wear, here we come," Cassidy said as they got back in the car. By now she'd decided that she really wanted a dress in midnight blue. Unfortunately, FRW didn't have many dresses in that color that were Cass's size.

"Maybe you need to be open to other colors." Mom held up a magenta gown that was in a style similar to what Cassidy had been looking for.

"Not that color." Cassidy just shook her head.

"How about black?" Mom held up another. "This one practically screams red carpet. Don't you think?"

Cassidy took that dress as well as several others in black and carried them back to the fitting room. But with each one she tried on, she began to feel more dejected. Mom was trying to be positive, suggesting that dresses could be taken in or let out or whatever. But Cassidy was just not seeing it.

"Why is this so hard?" she asked her mom.

Mom gave her a sympathetic smile. "I don't know, honey. I think you've looked gorgeous in a lot of the gowns."

"Maybe I should just settle for this one." Cassidy turned around in the black sleeveless gown.

"But you don't really like it, do you?"

"It's okay." Cassidy held the skirt out with a dismal smile.

"Take it off," Mom commanded. "Get dressed. I'm taking you to Macy's."

"Oh, Mom." Cassidy frowned. She was tired of shopping, tired of trying things on, and tired of prom dresses.

"Come on," Mom urged. "Just trust me, okay?"

Cassidy shrugged. "Okay."

Mom was obviously in her element at the big department store. She led Cassidy straight to where the racks of formal dresses were hanging and went into search mode. Meanwhile, Cassidy just watched, trying to feign interest as her mom perused the designer rack.

"How about this?" Mom held up a midnight-blue dress. "These rhinestones around the neckline would make it so you don't need much jewelry. And you can borrow a pair of my cubic zirconium earrings. The dangly ones would probably look nice on you."

Cassidy studied the shirred bodice and full skirt. "It'd be good for dancing."

"It's your size," Mom said enticingly.

"Do you think it will fit?"

"Only one way to find out." Mom started to guide Cassidy toward the fitting room.

To Cassidy's amazement, not only did it fit perfectly, it looked gorgeous. However, when she checked the price tag, she felt deflated. "It's too expensive," she called over the door. "It's $210, Mom. Way too much."

"Come out and show me the dress," Mom commanded.

Cassidy stepped out and Mom made an approving nod then reached for the price tag. "You read the *regular* price, Cass. All the designer formals are 40 percent off today. And then I get to use my 20 percent off coupon too."

Cassidy was doing the math in her head. "Hey, that's around a hundred dollars."

"That's right. Not that much more than a rental. And about the same as the nicer used gowns."

As Cassidy admired the dark color and soft, flowing fabric, she considered this. "Even less than some of the gowns."

"So what do you think?"

Cassidy spun around, making the skirt flow out. "I like it . . . but I feel kinda guilty."

"Guilty?" Mom frowned.

"Because it's a new dress . . . and Sofia . . ."

"But you can use your shoes from the Christmas ball and you don't need any accessories. That leaves a nice chunk of change to donate to Abby's fund for Sofia."

"That's true."

"Oh, Cass, you look so pretty." Mom smiled. "And you've

never been the kind of girl to splurge on fashion. Go ahead and do this, sweetie."

"Really?" Cassidy still felt unsure.

"Well, unless you want to keep shopping." Mom's eyes twinkled. "I suppose we could make a whole day of—"

"No, thanks." Cassidy shook her head.

"So is this the one?" Mom asked hopefully.

"I think so."

Mom chuckled as Cassidy returned to the changing room. "Not to say I told you so, honey, but if I'd had my way, we would've come here first and we'd have been done with our shopping hours ago."

Cassidy laughed as she removed the elegant gown. She really should've listened to her mom. Maybe the old saying was true—maybe mothers really did know best.

Bryn didn't know why she'd let her mom talk her into this stupid vacation during spring break. Oh sure, a girl getaway had sounded fun at first. But after a few days with Mom, Aunt Kristy, Aunt Lisa, and Grandma, Bryn was ready to go AWOL—not to mention totally nuts. Never mind that her two aunts fought almost constantly, or that her grandma seemed determined to fatten everyone up with all the high-calorie snacks she was constantly pushing at them, but the location of the "beach condo" was not exactly desirable. Besides feeling like a retirement home (the condo belonged to one of Grandma's elderly friends) the nearest shopping area was a forty-minute drive and, to Bryn's dismay, no one seemed very interested in going.

"Heading to the pool?" Mom asked as Bryn grabbed her beach bag and a bottle of water.

"I think I'll check out the beach."

"I'm sorry this hasn't been what you'd hoped," Mom said with a grimace.

"It's okay." Bryn forced a smile. "At least I can work on my tan today. That's something."

Mom patted Bryn's bare shoulder. "The weather hasn't been exactly accommodating, has it?"

"Not exactly." Bryn pushed open the sliding door. "But it's not your fault, Mom."

"Well, just a few more days, huh?"

Bryn just nodded. As she walked through the pool area, she tried to imagine how much more fun this week would've been if her DG friends had been here. She remembered how Devon had suggested they do some kind of spring break getaway. Maybe next year. At first Bryn had been pleased to hear that she and Mom were going to the beach condo. She'd even played it up when she'd told her friends.

But the truth was, as the week had progressed, she'd felt more and more envious of the other girls. From what she was hearing, they were all back home having a good time and busily preparing for prom. It sounded like Emma and her decorations committee were making great progress this week. Abby was monitoring her PBC blog and racking up lots of donations for the Sofia fund. And Devon had been successful at getting contributions from some of the local businesses. Bryn had also heard how Cass had gone dress shopping with her mom several days ago and managed to bag a totally cool dress at Macy's—and for around a hundred bucks. That in itself was encouraging since Bryn halfway expected all the DG girls to show up at prom wearing ill-fitting and sadly worn-out *used* gowns. At least Cass and Bryn would look good.

Of course, Bryn realized that without a date for prom,

she was destined to go with the girls' group that Cassidy had been helping to set up. Yes, it was a letdown. Not to mention lame. But Bryn had decided she would be a good sport and try to make the best of it. Because as of last Friday, it seemed that all the good guys were taken. It had been overwhelming to witness the promposals going off all over the school that day. The guys, it seemed, had been dropping like flies. But none of them dropped in front of Bryn.

"It's because pretty girls are intimidating," Devon had reassured Bryn on Friday. "Guys are afraid of rejection. That's why you should do what I did. Just swallow your pride and ask a guy yourself. No big deal."

Bryn had acted as if that was beneath her, but the truth was her confidence had been completely shot by then, and she honestly couldn't think of a guy to ask. She'd actually been relieved to run off with her mom on Saturday, although that had worn off pretty quickly. And that was seven long days ago.

Bryn sighed as she kicked off her sandals and walked on the warm sand. So far she had endured too many long days of watching the aunts consume too many margaritas and bicker like middle-school girls. Too many days of playing too many rummy games and working jigsaw puzzles while it rained and stormed outside. Five long evenings of watching too many chick flicks and eating too many of the fattening meals her grandma insisted on fixing. Bryn wondered if her prom gown would even fit her when she got home. Would there be time to have it altered again?

It felt like adding insult to injury to know that Abby, Emma, and Devon were going dress shopping together today. Bryn would give anything to be with them, but the best she could do was to keep her phone on and close at hand. She'd begged Abby to send photos of their final selections. "Not so I can approve your gowns," she'd assured Abby last night. "Just so I can see them." Then she'd confessed to her best friend that she was feeling pretty bummed this week. "This beach trip has been kinda disappointing." As she described the nasty weather and her crazy aunts, Abby had burst out laughing. "That does sound pretty sad." But at least she'd promised to send the photos.

Bryn laid out her towel on the sand and sat down. Really, she should be enjoying this. Today, although a bit breezy, was sunny. And the beach, which only had a few other sunbathers on it, was clean and pretty. But when her phone chimed, she completely forgot about her surroundings.

The first photo she saw was of Abby wearing a surprisingly pretty gown. Although it was sleeveless and cut in at the shoulders, the neckline was high, but because of Abby's long, slender neck, it looked really nice. And Bryn knew that Abby's rather conservative dad wouldn't have a problem with it. Plus that vibrant shade of coral looked stunning against Abby's dark skin tone.

Perfect, Bryn texted back. *Love it!*

Label says Badgley Mischka, Abby texted back. *Who?*

Bryn blinked in surprise then texted back. *A hot designer. How much?* Bryn knew a Mischka gown like that could not be cheap. What had happened to Abby's frugal plan?

$50.

Huh? Bryn texted back. Was that a typo? A Badgley Mischka couldn't possibly be that cheap.

Rental gown, Abby texted back.

Okay, that explained it. Not for the first time, Bryn wondered if perhaps she'd been all wrong about this whole rental-gown biz. Maybe it was silly—not to mention wasteful—to lay out that much money for a dress she'd only wear once. Especially when you don't even have a date! Bryn's cheeks grew warm as she considered this. And it wasn't from the sun.

After a bit, Abby sent the next photo. This one was of Emma in a frumpy-looking pale-blue gown. It was so bad that Bryn had to call, demanding to speak to Emma.

"Okay, first of all, I'm not saying this because that's almost the same color as my gown, Emma. But it really doesn't suit you at all. There's way too much fabric. You look lost in it."

"I know," Emma admitted. "It doesn't feel like me. Abby made me try it because it matches my eyes. I wanted to try on this black gown—it reminded me of something I saw on the red carpet, but Abby keeps saying I look better in pastels."

Bryn considered this. "Well, I agree that you do look good in pastels, Em. But you also look good in black—as long as you have a little blush and lip color to keep you from looking too faded. When it comes to dress designs, you need to look for something more fitted and narrower at the bottom—not fluffy or layered or full. Maybe a satin dress with a slit so that you can walk."

"Really?" Emma sounded hopeful. "That sounds like the black number I liked, but Devon and Abby said it looked too old for me."

"Let me see it," Bryn insisted.

"I'll go find it and put it on and send a picture."

Bryn felt slightly encouraged as she waited for Emma to send her the next photo. Okay, it wasn't as fun as being there, but it was better than playing another hand of gin rummy with Grandma.

Before long her phone chimed again and there was Emma in a sophisticated-looking black dress. Unfortunately, the neckline was way too low. Bryn started to text then decided to call. "I love everything about the dress," she began, "but the neckline is too plunging."

"I know. And it's a little big in the bust too." Emma laughed. "Or I'm a little small."

"Can they do some alteration?" Bryn asked. "It looks like you could shorten that V-neck by pulling it together on the bottom, Em. Can you get some straight pins and try to fasten it together just to see?"

Emma told someone what Bryn had said and it sounded like they were trying it out. "It works!" Emma exclaimed. "You should see it, Bryn."

"Send me another photo," Bryn insisted.

After a couple of minutes the next photo came and Bryn could see that it was much better. Still sleek and chic but not so much skin showing. And the design of the gown really made petite Emma look taller. *Beautiful*, Bryn texted back. *Perfect*.

The next time Bryn's phone rang it was Devon. "Where's your photo?" Bryn asked. "What's your dress look like?"

"I really need your help," Devon told her. "I've tried on a bunch of gowns and nothing looks right."

"Okay . . ." Bryn pictured Devon in her mind. Curvy redhead with a heart-shaped face. Mid-range height, mid-range weight. Sparkling dark-brown eyes. "What kind of look are you going for anyway?"

"That's the problem, I'm not sure. At first I thought I was going for black, kinda like what Emma picked out. But I tried one on and I looked like a hooker."

Bryn laughed. "Oh, I doubt that."

"Emma said I did."

"Hmm . . ." Bryn closed her eyes, trying to imagine what kind of dress would look great on Devon. "Well, you look fabulous in almost any shade of green," Bryn told her. "It really sets off your hair and your complexion."

"Okay . . . but what shade of green?"

"Probably something vibrant. Like a jewel tone. What about emerald?" Bryn opened her eyes to look out over the ocean. "Or even turquoise or teal."

"Teal?" Devon echoed. "There was a teal gown that caught my eye, but it's not exactly my usual look, you know?"

"Maybe that's a good thing. Try something different. Describe it."

"Well, the gown had a gathered skirt, and the bodice was cut like a strapless gown." She laughed. "Which would probably look hot on me. But then it had this lace thingy going on up above the bodice. I mean, the lace part was the same color as the dress, but you could see skin through it. But it was kind of, well, modest, I guess you'd say." She laughed harder now.

"Go try it on," Bryn commanded. "And send me the photo." In Bryn's opinion, Devon would do well to consider less flashy styles. With all her curvy flamboyance, that girl often pushed it too far. And Em was right, Devon needed to be careful or she could look like a hooker. Anyway, it would be interesting to see her in a "modest" gown.

When Devon's photo popped up, Bryn was totally shocked. Devon looked amazing in this dress. And although the neckline was high and the little cap sleeves covered her shoulders, Devon still looked hot. But it was a good sort of hot. Once again, Bryn decided to just call her. "I love that dress," she told Devon. "You look like a million bucks in it. Very classic and chic."

"Really?"

"Absolutely. It's gorgeous and if you don't get it, I'll be seriously disappointed in you."

"The other girls are gaga over it too," Devon conceded. "So I guess this wraps it up."

"Is Felicia with you?" Bryn asked.

"No, she's visiting Sofia."

"Oh . . . How is Sofia?"

Devon sighed. "Sounds like she's in a lot of pain."

"Poor thing."

"But Felicia said to tell you she took your advice on her gown," Devon continued. "I think Emma might have a photo on her phone."

"Tell her to send it to me," Bryn said before she hung up. She'd known that Felicia was worried about her prom dress. Bryn had done a long online search trying to find some gowns that would look great on Felicia, but not be too over-the-top for her parents. Like Abby's dad, the Ruezes were fairly conservative—especially after what had happened with Felicia last winter when she'd suddenly decided to sneak some rather strange items of clothing to school, behind her mom's back.

Bryn's phone chimed again. This time the message was from Emma, and the photo was of a smiling Felicia wearing a gown that looked almost identical to one of the images that Bryn had sent her more than a week ago. It was a sleeveless gown with a hot pink bodice—a jewel neckline that was modest enough to please any dad—and a flowing skirt in a bright colored print of orange and coral and hot pink. Kind of a tropical look, but with Felicia's brown skin and shiny black hair, it looked amazing . . . and expensive. But when Bryn questioned Emma on the price, Emma informed her that the dress came from Formal Rental Wear and had only cost forty bucks. Go figure!

Devon didn't normally consider herself a particularly generous person. Okay, that was probably an understatement. She secretly felt that she was extremely selfish and narcissistic. After all, hadn't her own mother said as much? And more than once. Lots more than once. When Devon was thirteen or fourteen she'd decided she needed to look out for the big number one. Herself. Because, really, who else would? And if, as a result, she came across as self-serving and egotistical, well, that was her problem, right? Until it was no longer right. Until it became clear that it was actually wrong. Very wrong.

Devon wasn't exactly sure how to explain what had been going on inside her these past several months. More specifically since she'd been enrolled, against her will, into Northwood Academy and since the Dating Games club had been established. She knew the changes in her weren't the result of participating in a "dating club." In reality, the club had always been more about the girls—and the friendships—than it had ever been about dating or guys. Ironic, since the latter had been Devon's primary purpose when she'd instigated the club back in September. Live and learn.

Anyway, it was for these reasons—and lots of other reasons that Devon couldn't quite put her finger on—that she was determined to do something for Bryn. As Abby's mom drove them home from their prom shopping trip, Devon decided to bring it up.

"I think we should put together a promposal for Bryn," she announced from the backseat where she and Emma were sitting.

"Huh?" Emma looked confused. "You mean we're going to invite Bryn to prom?"

"No." Devon shook her head. "We're going to call up Darrell Zuckerman and—"

"Darrell Zuckerman?" Abby said from the front seat. "Are you serious?"

"Hey, if I can go to prom with Leonard, why can't Bryn go with Darrell?"

"Who's Darrell?" Abby's mom asked quietly.

"A kid at school," Abby told her.

"A kinda nerdy kid," Emma filled in.

"But he's nice," Abby assured her mom. "And he took Bryn to the masquerade ball."

"And I think they actually had a pretty good time," Emma added.

"Bryn handled it better than I did," Devon confessed.

The car got quiet, and Devon figured her friends were just doing her a favor by not rubbing her nose in the fact that she'd treated poor Leonard like doggy doo.

"So are you girls saying that Bryn does not have a date for prom?" Abby's mom sounded surprised.

"Yeah," Abby told her. "I think it's because girls like Bryn can be intimidating. She probably could've gone with Jason, but she really doesn't like him. In fact, none of us are too fond of him."

"He's kind of a jerk," Emma said quietly.

"Yeah." Devon agreed. "Anyway . . . I got this idea. I mean, even though Bryn says she's okay about going to prom with the girls' group, she still sounds pretty bummed about not having a date. So here's what I'm thinking. What if we helped Darrell put together a really good promposal for Bryn?"

"Darrell making a promposal?" Abby sounded skeptical.

"We would help him," Devon clarified. "We could figure something out—something fun and different—and Darrell could do it on Monday."

"I like it," Emma said. "And Bryn's been such a good sport. It would be nice if she had a date for prom."

"Do you guys have any ideas?" Devon asked. "I mean, it seems like almost everything's been done. It would be fun to see Darrell do something different."

"I had an idea," Abby said suddenly. "I was actually day-dreaming about doing it for Kent." She laughed. "Fortunately, he beat me to the punch." She explained her idea of putting together a flash dance.

"I'd love to be in a flash dance," Devon said eagerly. "I was on dance team at my other high school."

"Maybe you could help choreograph it," Abby suggested.

"You could help her," Abby's mom said. "You took a lot of dance classes when you were younger."

"Yeah . . . well."

"Great," Devon said quickly. "Abby, you can help me."

Before long, it was decided that Devon would figure out the music and then she'd meet with Abby after track practice tomorrow, and the two of them would create a flash dance plan.

"Hopefully we can get the whole DG to help," Devon said. "Well, except for Bryn. Let's keep this from her until Monday."

"Maybe we could have a sleepover with the DG," Abby suggested. "That way we could go over the flash dance until everyone's got it down."

"Perfect," Devon agreed.

"But it would be really cool if we could get some guys involved too," Abby said. "That's the way I'd imagined it."

"We might be able to get some of the youth group guys on Saturday night," Emma suggested.

"If we keep their steps simple and leave the more complicated choreography for the DG, well, it might actually work," Abby said.

"We have to get Darrell to do something," Devon added. "Maybe he could dress up somehow."

By the time Abby's mom dropped off Devon, they had the beginnings of what seemed like a very good plan. A plan that they all swore to keep top secret from Bryn.

• • ● • •

By Monday morning, Devon was very excited to get to school. In fact, she couldn't remember the last time she'd looked forward to a school day like this. They'd spent the last several days putting together what might just be the best promposal yet. Even Darrell Zuckerman had gotten fully on board. Devon couldn't wait until noon, when the flash dance would be revealed to everyone in the cafeteria. Until then, Devon and the others had to act totally nonchalant. The fun in this plan would be to catch Bryn totally off guard. And Isaac had been assigned to get the whole thing on camera.

Finally, lunchtime came. The DG, as always, were sitting at their usual table—but this time with a totally oblivious Bryn. They were all talking like normal when the music started—a peppy song from the Red Hot Chili Peppers—and suddenly all the DG girls except Bryn jumped to their feet, and the flash dance began.

Even Felicia, thanks to Emma's help, was participating, and as they circled out and back in again, closing in around Bryn, Devon could tell that Bryn was totally bewildered. Then the youth group guys jumped in, and there were about a dozen dancing altogether, all rocking out to the song. As planned, the girls faded back and the guys stepped in front. Just like Devon had asked, all the guys had jackets on over the white T-shirts that had been provided by the girls.

As the tempo got livelier, Darrell Zuckerman appeared. Dressed in an old tuxedo he'd borrowed from a relative, he danced through the circle of girls and into the center of the guys. When the music abruptly stopped, the guys, one by one going down the line, all opened their jackets to expose the letters that had been taped in red onto the white T-shirts:

P-R-O-M-?

Darrell dropped to one knee, holding out his hand to Bryn. Her expression was hard to read, and for a moment Devon was concerned. What if Bryn said no thanks? But then to everyone's relief, Bryn burst into laughter and, grasping Darrell's hand, yelled out, "Yes! Most definitely."

Everyone clapped and cheered and laughed. When the music started up again, it seemed like everyone wanted to dance. Devon wasn't sure if it was the most spectacular promposal yet, but she thought it was probably the most fun. Even if it was a little bit last-minute.

• • ● • •

Bryn had never experienced so many different emotions in such a short period of time. At first she was confused. What were her friends doing? Then she thought she was hallucinating. How could they possibly dance that fabulously without her knowing about it? As the dance grew bigger and better, she felt slightly left out. Like she'd been stuck at the beach with the old girls' group for way too long. Finally, when she discovered it was all being done for her, she was just plain flabbergasted and slightly speechless.

It wasn't until she saw Darrell Zuckerman, looking surprisingly suave in a Mad Men sort of tuxedo and making his way toward her, that it all started to make some kind of sense. Then all the guys ripped open their jackets to reveal those lovely big red letters inviting her to prom, and Darrell got down on one knee. Well, what else could she say? Besides, she *wanted* to go to prom with him. He was a really good dancer.

After the hubbub surrounding the unexpected flash dance died down, Bryn asked her friends who was the brains behind this amazing occurrence.

The girls just shrugged, giving Bryn blank looks. Finally

Emma jerked her thumb toward Devon. "It was her idea to do a promposal."

"Seriously?" Bryn stared at Devon in wonder.

"But Abby helped with the choreography," Devon explained. "Everyone jumped in after that."

"It was really fun," Abby told Bryn.

"We wanted to make sure you had a date," Cassidy said.

"After all, the DG is about dating," Felicia reminded Bryn.

Bryn knew that she'd probably taken her friendship with these girls for granted, but today it seemed to mean more to her than ever. "I have an idea," she told them as the lunch hour was ending. "Let's all meet at my house before prom. We can all get ready there and help each other. And then we can do a sleepover after prom. Okay?"

Everyone agreed that sounded like fun. As Bryn went to class, she was determined to make prom night as much about her friends as it was about prom.

• • • • •

There was lots to do before Saturday night, and as chair of the prom committee, Bryn had her hands full. On Tuesday she held an "emergency" prom committee meeting. "I'll give you the good news . . . and the bad news," she began. "According to Mrs. Dorman, this prom has sold more tickets than any other prom in Northwood history."

The committee members applauded and exchanged congrats.

"The bad news is that, as a result of the high attendance, we're short on some things." She glanced at her notes. "Thanks to several restaurants and Northwood's own culinary arts program, we've got enough cooks and chefs to prepare the dinner. And Le Chateau has graciously upgraded us to their large banquet room. Thankfully, it was free. But we are severely shorthanded on waitstaff. Mrs. Dorman has arranged for me to go make an appeal to the eighth graders at Northwood Middle. Hopefully we'll get some volunteers. But if anyone else has connections—friends from your church or family members—please let me know."

"What about food?" someone asked. "Hopefully we won't be short on that. Those dinner tickets aren't exactly cheap and I know people are expecting a good meal before prom."

"That's a good question and we need to work on it," Bryn told them. "Mrs. Dorman and I came up with an idea to help stretch what we've had donated. We're sending home a flyer today, putting out a call to the Northwood parents, inviting them to sign up online to donate appetizers and desserts. The flyer will remind parents that all prom proceeds are going to help Sofia Ruez. Hopefully that will help to ignite their interest."

Bryn went over more details, assigning more housekeeping tasks and fielding more questions. By the time the meeting broke up, she felt reassured that she had a good team. Everyone seemed to care about making prom a success. She knew the whole promposal thing had a lot to do with that. For some reason the silly antics of people making public promposals had really bolstered school spirit and morale. Everyone felt certain that was why so many kids wanted to go to prom. That and the fact that they'd opened it up to the sophomore and freshman classes.

On Wednesday morning, Bryn visited Northwood Academy's eighth grade class to make an appeal to the kids there. She used the poster with Sofia's photograph as her visual aid, first telling them about the young girl's battle against leukemia and her need for good but expensive treatment. Then she explained how the prom proceeds would all go to help Sofia Ruez, and how every dollar made would be matched. Finally she reminded the eighth graders that next year they would be students at high school and prom would eventually be their responsibility. And to her relief, about thirty kids signed up to help. Probably more than they needed, but it would be better to have too many than too few.

"You'll need to wear black pants and white shirts." She explained the rest of the details as she handed out the permission releases for their parents to sign. "And you'll report an hour early for a quick training session." She smiled. "We really appreciate it!"

As Bryn drove back to the high school, she felt a real sense of accomplishment. It was no small feat organizing an event like this. The experience she'd gotten during the school year working on similar events had proved to be good training for this one. She knew this role would look good on her college résumé. And who knew, maybe someday she'd want to work full time as an events planner. That is, if her future in the fashion industry didn't pan out.

With the help of the decorations committee and a few other volunteers, Emma spent more than six hours getting the decorations set up over at Le Chateau. The cordoned-off red carpet was laid out, complete with large golden stars that glistened in the white lights stretched between the little brass posts. The big gold-and-silver heart-shaped balloon sculpture with more little white lights twisted through was all set and ready for photos. Everywhere you looked in the ballroom, as well as the banquet room, was a glittering display of gold stars, white lights, sparkle, and splash—all the touches of glitz and glamour that represented Hollywood. Very elegant and inviting. All that was missing was girls in gowns and guys in tuxes . . . and that was only a few hours away.

"Thanks for helping," Emma told Devon and Cassidy as they walked through the hotel lobby. Her friends had rushed to her aid a couple hours ago when she'd put out the call for help. "I'd probably still be wearing my jeans right now if you guys hadn't come to my rescue."

"Poor Cinderella," Cassidy teased, "you wouldn't be able to attend the ball."

Devon paused by the front door, pointing to the area that the hotel had let the school use to display the promposal prize. The shiny red bike and backpack and camping gear, along with a prominent sign from the sporting goods store, were all neatly arranged. "Bryn and I set it up this morning," Devon explained. "It was my idea to add all the helium balloons. And the way I tied them to the bike would make it really hard for someone to steal it."

"Hopefully no one would do that," Cass said.

"It's a great prize and it looks really good," Emma told Devon. "Makes me wish I'd tried to win it myself."

Devon reached under the cordon to straighten the backpack against the wheel of the bike, making it stand up better. "There."

"So who do you think will win it?" Cassidy asked as they went out to get her car.

"Not Isaac." Emma laughed to remember the mocha cup with the word *Prom?* penned onto the side. The slightly worn cup now held a place of honor on her bedroom dresser.

"Probably not Lane either," Cassidy said. "Although his song is still going through my head."

"Probably because you look at the video every night before you go to bed," Devon teased.

Cass laughed. "Yeah, as a matter of fact."

"Well, I've spent a fair amount of time looking at the promposal site myself," Devon admitted. "There are some really good entries. I'm not feeling as optimistic as I did before."

"Well, if there was an early bird prize, you would've won it," Emma assured her.

"Yeah, and it was nice that you sort of got the ball rolling," Cassidy said as they got into the car. "And no offense, Devon, but I voted for Darrell."

"Me too," Emma confessed. "And the truth is I've actually watched that flash dance about ten times. It's so awesome!"

"I know," Cass said. "But I still felt a tiny bit guilty. I mean, maybe I should've voted for Lane. Especially considering that sweet song he did for me. But I was just trying to be fair . . . voting for the best."

"I voted for Darrell too," Devon told them.

"Wouldn't that be awesome if he won?" Emma said. "Kind of like we won too."

"Only he'd get the bike," Devon pointed out. "And even though we did most of the work for the dance, Darrell was such a good sport."

"And the way he looked in that cool vintage tux, and his attitude . . . ," Emma added. "Darrell made it what it is. He deserves it."

"Besides that, I doubt that Darrell's high school days have been exactly memorable—I mean, in a good way," Cassidy said.

"But taking Bryn to prom," Emma said, "that should be a pretty good memory. At least I hope it is."

"So . . . who did you guys vote for—I mean, for prom queen?" Devon asked as Cassidy parked in front of Bryn's house.

No one said a word. But Emma, remembering how Devon

could sometimes get a little full of herself, got worried. Surely Devon wouldn't think she had a chance to win the prom queen title. Besides this being her first year at Northwood, Devon had managed to make almost as many enemies as friends at this school.

"Okay, fine," Devon said as they got out of the car and started gathering up their prom stuff. "I probably shouldn't be so nosy. But I might as well tell you that I voted for Bryn. I mean, think about it—if she hadn't done all that she's done on prom committee and getting the whole promposal thing going, well, prom might not have even happened this year."

Emma gave Devon a relieved smile. "I voted for Bryn too."

"Me too." Cassidy chuckled. "But let's not tell her, okay?"

"Yeah," Emma agreed. "Let's not get her hopes up. Especially since Amanda Norton was really going for it."

"You'd think if she was really going for it, she'd have tried to be more helpful on prom committee," Cass said. "Mostly she's had excuses."

"Well, I know that Jason's been campaigning hard for Amanda," Emma told them. "Isaac said he's been pressuring all the guys."

"Probably because he wants to dance with the prom queen," Devon pointed out.

"Chances are, he will. And Amanda's a senior," Cassidy reminded them. "That's an advantage."

"Too bad they don't do prom princess for second place," Emma said wistfully. "I'll bet Bryn could've won that for sure."

As they lugged their bags and things up to the house, they changed the subject from prom queen to transportation. "I can't believe we're going to prom in a stretch limo," Devon said. "What's up with that?"

"Yeah, that's what Lane told me too." Cassidy set a bag down on the porch. "But what about saving money?"

"I thought the same thing," Emma replied. "But Felicia told me that Marcus got the limo for free since his uncle owns the company. He only has to pay for gas."

"Speaking of Marcus, is Felicia coming?" Devon asked.

"Yeah." Emma rang the doorbell. "But not until later. Her mom wants her to get dressed at home so they can take pictures and stuff there."

"But Bryn said all the parents were welcome to come here."

"I know. But Felicia's mom has to get back to the cancer center for Sofia and—"

"Welcome!" Bryn exclaimed as she opened the door wide. "Come on in. Abby's already here." She led them down to the basement where everything was set up for facials and manicures. After everyone had enjoyed those, they helped each other with hair and makeup. They were just finishing up when Felicia arrived.

"You look gorgeous," Bryn exclaimed as Felicia glided down the stairs in her festive-looking gown.

"Who did your hair?" Devon asked as she checked out Felicia's sleek updo.

"My aunt," Felicia said. "Do you think it makes me look too old? That's what Dad said."

"No, you look beautiful," Emma assured her.

"But where are your gowns?" Felicia frowned at their casual attire. "It's almost time for the boys to get here."

"We were just about to get dressed." Cassidy removed the plastic bag from her dark-blue gown.

After taking a few minutes for everyone to get into their prom dresses, they marched upstairs to take photos. They took some shots in the house and some out in Bryn's pretty backyard. Before long, the stretch limo with six dapper guys bearing wrist corsages arrived, followed by a number of parents who wanted to sneak a peek at the prom-goers and snag some pictures.

Bryn's mom had put out a nice spread of appetizers and beverages, which were rapidly diminished once the guys got over seeing their dates. And there was no denying that every girl in the DG looked fabulous. No wardrobe malfunctions. No hairdo don'ts. No makeup mistakes. Even the colors of their gowns seemed to complement each other. And for the first time in the short history of the DG dates, everyone was getting along nicely. Even the guys were being friendly to each other. That was greatly appreciated considering that Darrell and Leonard weren't regulars with the other guys.

All in all, Emma thought this prom had the potential to be the best date of the year—just like they all had hoped it would be. And although everyone kept saying there was no hurry to rush off to Le Chateau since their dinner reservation wasn't until seven, it was obvious that they were all somewhat eager to go. Not just to get out on the dance floor, but probably to find out who'd won the promposal contest.

Of course, there was good-natured rivalry in the limo. Everyone was acting like they should win the promposal prize. Well, everyone except Darrell. He seemed content to just listen.

"So you're saying my coffee cup won't cut it?" Isaac was teasing Devon.

"I'm saying my Juliet beats out your coffee cup by miles," she tossed back.

"I liked it," Leonard chimed in. "Although I was pretty shocked at the time."

"Well, I happen to like my coffee cup invite," Emma told Isaac. "Understated, but to the point."

"What about my pizza?" Kent asked Abby. "It might not have been all splashy and flashy, but it sure hit the spot."

"That's right," Abby agreed. "I would've much rather had a pizza than a flash dance. We'd had a hard practice that day."

Cassidy smiled at Lane. "Well, I hate to say it, but I don't think you have much of a chance to win the bike—but I still think your song was awesome."

"Hey, did you ever get those words off your chest?" Felicia asked Marcus.

He laughed. "You can still see traces of it. Man, I can't believe I trusted my kid sister. She swore it was water-based ink before she penned it onto me."

They all laughed.

• • ● • •

Because of the unprecedented ticket sales for prom and the somewhat limited seating space in the banquet hall, prom-goers had to make reservations for dinner between 6:30 and 8:30. And since the winners of the promposal contest as well as prom queen would be announced at eight, everyone in the DG group had opted to eat at seven. That would give them plenty of time to enjoy dinner before the big announcement.

As the meal progressed, Abby noticed that Bryn was being relatively quiet. But not in a sulky way. In fact, she seemed refreshingly pleasant. And whenever she did contribute something it seemed to be more thoughtful than usual . . . or maybe less self-centered. Abby wasn't even exactly sure what the difference was, but something about her best friend did seem different. In a good way.

"So all the food was donated from businesses?" Kent asked Bryn.

"Everything in the main course," she explained. "The appetizers and desserts were made by Northwood parents."

Darrell held up his fork. "Well, my compliments to the chef. This prime rib is delicious."

"And so is the fish," Lane added.

"What do you guys think of our young servers?" Bryn asked. "Don't they look cute in their black pants and white shirts?"

"They look great," Abby told her. "Where'd you get all the black ties?"

"My grandma made them by sewing strips of fabric," Bryn explained.

"Nice touch," Darrell told Bryn.

"Well, for a frugal prom, this is looking pretty good," Lane said.

It was about 7:45 when they finished their desserts and, seeing that there were other kids waiting to eat, Abby suggested that they vacate their table.

"Good idea," Bryn agreed. "Gives us time to visit the little girls' room before they announce the promposal winner." She held crossed fingers up to Darrell. "Not that I'm holding my breath." She giggled.

The ladies' room was already crowded with girls, including Amanda Norton and her entourage of friends, who were monopolizing the largest portion of mirror space in the waiting room section of the restroom. These girls were dressed to the nines and, although Abby would never reveal this to anyone, she knew for a fact that none of those girls had participated in her Prom Budget Challenge. She was guessing, by their appearance as well as their conversation, that these girls had shelled out some serious money on their gowns and accessories.

The DG girls went past them into the main part of the bathroom, where they managed to secure a sink and a corner of the mirror, taking turns to freshen up, reapply lip gloss, and check their teeth for food. But as Abby went into the other section of the bathroom in search of a tissue to blot her lip gloss, which was starting to bleed, she couldn't help but overhear Amanda and her friends.

"Don't worry," Sienna was quietly reassuring Amanda. "You're *going* to win. Everyone says so."

Amanda smoothed her glossy blonde hair, then shrugged with an air of nonchalance. "Well, that's what Jason says too, but you never know."

"We know," another one of her friends said.

"It's in the bag," Rebecca Proctor added. "Trust us. We've got you covered."

Abby frowned as she paused in the doorway. What made these girls so certain of that? She wanted to question them, but knowing it could start something unpleasant, she decided to keep her mouth shut. Just grab a tissue and beat it.

"Eavesdropping, are we?" Rebecca asked Abby.

Abby blinked as she reached for a facial tissue. "No, I just needed this." To prove her point, she leaned toward the mirror and adjusted her lip gloss. Abby was well aware that Rebecca was no fan of the DG. For that matter, Amanda wasn't either. But really, wasn't that all water under the bridge by now? Abby thought that these girls, all seniors, would've gotten beyond childish bickering . . . and hopefully grown up some. But maybe she was wrong. Maybe some people never grew up.

"Can you believe that anyone would actually *rent* a dress?" Rebecca asked her friends. Naturally they laughed.

"It's kind of creepy to imagine wearing a gown that someone else wore," Amanda said. "I mean, who knows what they might've done in it."

"Eww." Rebecca wrinkled her nose. "Let's not even go there."

Abby knew their jabs were meant for her and, despite her earlier resolve, she couldn't stop herself. "I'm curious," she said, "what makes you so certain that Amanda's going to be crowned queen?"

Amanda gave Abby an innocent look. "Who said that?"

"Your friends." Abby remained planted in the doorway, although she could tell that some of the girls were standing behind her now. Probably listening.

"Well, some things are just obvious," Sienna told Abby.

"Yeah," Rebecca said, "as obvious as used dresses."

More laughter.

Abby stood up straighter. "You know, I honestly feel sorry for you guys."

"You're sorry for us?" Amanda asked.

Abby nodded. "It seems like you missed out on what was really special about this prom." She waved to their expensive dresses. "Sure, it was your choice not to save some money to help a little girl's battle with cancer. No one can make you do what you don't want to. But the funny thing is that those of us who did it—the girls who had the confidence to wear a gently used gown—we're not just having fun because we're at prom, we're having fun because we know we're making a difference in a little girl's life. I think you've missed out on that. And I honestly feel sorry for you."

"We're here, aren't we?" Amanda challenged. "At least we came to prom. And the cost of our prom tickets will go to the Ruez girl, right?"

"That's true," Abby conceded, resisting the urge to point out that their dates had probably covered that expense. "But I didn't notice you in the banquet room. Then again, maybe you haven't eaten yet."

"We already had an amazing dinner," Sienna told her. Then she went into detail about the very expensive restaurant where they'd just eaten.

"So you could've contributed even more to the Sofia fund if you'd wanted. But once again you chose not to." Abby sadly shook her head. "It's your decision, but I do feel sorry for you. You won't get to enjoy prom like we will—with the knowledge that we've really helped someone in need. That's pretty cool." She shrugged. "That's all I'm saying."

"Well, we'll enjoy ourselves when we celebrate Amanda as prom queen," Rebecca said a bit slyly. "And from what I hear, Jason's got that promposal prize nailed too."

Abby frowned. "Just where are you getting your information anyway?"

Rebecca's brows arched. "Oh, I don't reveal my sources."

"Let's just say a little bird told us." Sienna giggled.

"Come on, Abs." Cassidy firmly linked arms with Abby. "Let's get out of here."

"Yeah," Devon agreed, coming along the other side. "I'm in need of some fresh air."

Just like that, all the DG girls surrounded Abby and guided her out of the ladies' room, almost as if they thought she was some kind of timed explosive device that was about to go off. And perhaps they were right. Maybe she was. But as soon as they were out in the big space in the lobby, Abby felt herself relax. She smiled at her friends, thanking them for rescuing her. As the girls strolled toward the ballroom, where their dates were waiting by the entrance, Abby knew that what she'd said to Amanda and her friends was absolutely true. She did feel sorry for them. It was as if they were missing the whole point. But really, what can you do?

Cassidy was relieved to see that Abby was calmer now. She'd heard enough of the bathroom conversation to know that Amanda and her friends had been "politely" goading Abby. Just the same, Cassidy respected Abby for standing her ground and speaking the truth . . . without losing her cool.

"There they are," Kent announced as the six girls joined their dates. He peered curiously at Abby. "Everything okay?"

"Abby was just trying to reeducate some snobs," Devon told him as she linked her arm into Leonard's. "Some people are so snooty."

Cassidy suppressed the urge to laugh. She remembered a time—months ago—when Devon could have fallen into the snooty category. Fortunately, she'd been changing a lot. Too bad Amanda and her friends hadn't.

"Ready to go in?" Lane held out his arm to Cassidy.

"Yes." She linked her arm in his. "Let's do this."

The other couples paired off too and, as a group, they all walked into the room. With all the lights on and everything in its place, the ballroom was amazingly enchanting. "Oh, Emma," Cassidy called over her shoulder. "It's beautiful. You did a great job."

The others complimented Emma too, and before long, they were all taking turns posing in front of the big silver-and-gold balloon star, having their photos taken with their dates. Bryn asked the photographer if the whole DG could get a group shot. He gladly agreed, and all six girls squeezed into the center of the star. Hamming it up, they all said cheese.

"In case I didn't already tell you," Lane said quietly in Cassidy's ear as the girls rejoined the guys, "you look really beautiful tonight."

"Thanks. I think you mentioned it a time . . . or three." Cassidy laughed. Not for the first time, she was glad that Mom had talked her into this fabulous dress. She knew it was a splurge and slightly out of character for her usual no-nonsense style, but she also knew—thanks to Dad—how much she was able to contribute to Sofia's fund. And, like Abby had tried to tell Amanda and her friends, that felt good.

A new song started and Lane and Cassidy, as well as their friends, crowded onto the dance floor and started to dance. A couple of songs later, Cassidy was starting to wonder about the time. It had to be past eight by now. Wasn't Mr. Worthington supposed to go up and announce the promposal winner and prom queen?

Cassidy had noticed Amanda and her entourage coming into the ballroom a few minutes ago. She hated to feel judgmental, but after overhearing those girls with Abby in the bathroom and seeing the way they walked into the room just now—like they owned the place—well, it was a little aggravating. Still, she was determined to not let it get to her. And it seemed like her friends—including Abby—had already moved on. Even Bryn looked like she was having the time of her life as she and Darrell danced. Cassidy had almost forgotten what a good dancer Darrell had proven himself to be at the masquerade ball. And in that same vintage suit that he'd worn for the promposal, he looked very debonair . . . and cool. Maybe Darrell's nerd days were behind him now.

"Attention, attention!" Mr. Worthington was on the stage now, speaking into the mike as the music faded. "It's time for some very special announcements." He waited as the room slowly grew quiet and everyone circled around the stage, waiting for him to continue.

"As you all must know, this is a very special sort of prom—a first for Northwood Academy." He smiled over the crowd. "I can't begin to tell you how proud I am of all of you. The way you've all reached out, opening your arms and your hearts, as well as your pocketbooks, to help one of our student's families—well, I hardly have words to express how pleased that makes me." He waved over to where Mrs. Dorman was waiting with the prom queen crown on a velvet pillow. "Come on over here. Before we announce the vote results, I want Mrs. Dorman to share something."

He held the mike for her, waiting for her to speak. "I agree with what Mr. Worthington just said. This has been a truly amazing prom. And I want to acknowledge the prom committee, which was headed by Bryn Jacobs. You all did an outstanding job. Above and beyond anything we've ever seen before—and beyond anything we ever imagined possible." She beamed at them. "And now the good news is this—as a result of all your fund-raising energies, including matching funds from a generous family foundation, this year's prom has miraculously raised nearly fifty thousand dollars."

The whole room erupted in loud cheers and clapping that went on for nearly a minute.

Mr. Worthington acted as if he was about to faint, wiping a hand across his forehead. "I am in total shock," he told them. "It doesn't seem possible." He waved his arms toward the crowd. "But it is thanks to you—all of you. Your hard work and your sacrifice have just helped young Sofia Ruez in her battle against leukemia."

Cassidy looked over at Felicia. With Marcus on one side and Emma on the other, almost as if they were supporting her from falling, Felicia had tears streaming down her cheeks. She was holding her phone in a trembling hand, and Cassidy suspected that Felicia was texting her parents the amazing news.

"And now to announce the results from the vote," Mr. Worthington said in a slightly more solemn tone. "Unfortunately, we had some challenges with our online ballot box. But we got a computer expert to look into it, and after a recount, we're ready to announce the results." He cleared his throat. "First of all, for the winner of that great-looking mountain bike. I wouldn't mind having one of those myself—but for the promposal that received the most votes, the prize goes to Darrell Zuckerman."

Once again the crowd burst into cheers and applause. And

Darrell waved and made mock bows, playing it up for their enjoyment.

"And now for the young lady voted to reign over this year's prom," Mr. Worthington said solemnly. "I am pleased and proud to announce it's the very same young lady who has worked so tirelessly to make this prom such a success. Bryn Jacobs, please come up here and receive your crown."

Bryn looked truly shocked. But Darrell, hardly missing a beat, linked his arm in hers and escorted her up to the stage. Mrs. Dorman secured the crown onto Bryn's head and Mr. Worthington presented her with a bouquet of pink roses, then handed her the mike. "We'd like to hear a few words from our queen."

"Oh, my!" Bryn took in a raspy breath. "Thank you, everyone. This is so amazing. I don't even know what to say." She paused as if to steady herself. "But this crown should belong to all of you—everyone who helped to make this prom what it is, the ones who worked and sacrificed . . . I thank you. And in a hospital a few hours from here there's a little girl who I expect wants to thank you as well." She pointed to the crown. "This one's for Sofia."

Once again, everyone clapped and cheered. As Darrell escorted Bryn down the steps, the music began to play, and while the others watched, Darrell and Bryn performed a really stellar dance in the middle of the floor.

• • ● • •

All six girls were in high spirits when they finally got to Bryn's house around midnight. Really, could the evening have been more perfect? Oh, sure, there was that little glitch with Amanda and her friends in the ladies' room. But hearing the total of the money that had been raised for Sofia and seeing Bryn crowned queen, well, everyone agreed that it totally made up for the Amanda factor. And no one was terribly surprised or very sorry when Amanda and her entourage left the prom early.

As the girls removed their pretty gowns and got into comfortable sweats and shorts and sleepwear, Devon asked if they were going to play "rate your date" like they'd done in the past. But everyone agreed there was no need for that this time. All their dates would've received top scores tonight.

"Even Leonard," Devon proclaimed. "He was a true gentleman."

"And Darrell was fantastic," Bryn said. "What a dancer!"

They ate the junk food provided by Bryn and talked for a while about their dates and the evening in general. Then Felicia, who'd been rather quiet since they'd gotten home, finally spoke up.

"You guys are amazing," she said with a sweet intensity. "Truly amazing. When I think of how you all became my friends last winter . . . and the way you helped me out of that mess . . . and then the way you've helped Sofia by raising so much money tonight . . ." With tears in her eyes, she slowly shook her head. "I just cannot believe it."

Emma put an arm around Felicia's shoulders.

"My parents cannot believe it," Felicia continued. "What you have done for Sofia really may mean the difference between life and death. My mom was getting ready to remove her from the cancer treatment center—and it was really sad because Sofia has made so many good friends there. But because of your gift, she can stay—hopefully until she is well. I'm so thankful."

"We're not done. We'll think of more ways to raise money," Bryn assured Felicia. "We have over a month of school left. Who knows what we can raise by then?"

"That's right," Abby chimed in. "We're not done yet. Not by any means."

"And even though prom was the last big date of the school year . . . and the school year will be over in a few weeks . . . ," Cassidy spoke tentatively, "well, I just hope we're not done with the DG. I'd hate to see it end."

"Of course not," Emma declared. "Besides, as we all know, the DG isn't only about dating guys."

"That's for sure," Bryn agreed. "If it was, I'd have to say it's been less than a huge success. Four dates in the course of a whole school year isn't exactly record setting."

"Maybe not," Devon said quietly. "I might've thought that at first. But I know now that the DG is about us—about being friends. In fact, I was just thinking that 'DG' might stand for something completely different."

"What?" they all demanded.

"It's going to sound really lame," Devon said. "Like I've been spending too much time with Grandma Betty."

Emma shook a finger at Devon. "Hey, watch what you say about—"

"I love Grandma Betty," Devon assured her. "But she says some funny things sometimes."

Emma nodded. "So what does 'DG' stand for?"

Devon grinned at them. "*Dear Girls*." She laughed. "That's what Grandma Betty calls me sometimes, *dear girl*. Sometimes it's in exasperation, and other time it's just really sweet. But I got to thinking that is exactly what you guys are to me. *Dear*

Girls. But don't tell anyone I said that, okay? Maybe we can keep that to ourselves."

"I like it," Abby proclaimed. "Dear Girls."

Bryn held up her soda can. "Here's to *Dear Girls*." They all held up their drinks, echoing her toast as they clicked their cans together. "Here's to the real DG."

MELODY CARLSON is the award-winning author of over two hundred books, including *The Jerk Magnet*, *The Best Friend, The Prom Queen*, *Double Take*, and the Diary of a Teenage Girl series. Melody recently received a *Romantic Times* Career Achievement Award in the inspirational market for her books. She and her husband live in Central Oregon. For more information about Melody, visit her website at www.melodycarlson.com.

Meet Melody at

MelodyCarlson.com

- Enter a contest for a signed book
- Read her monthly newsletter
- Find a special page for book clubs
- Discover more books by Melody

Become a fan on Facebook